Adjusting Focus

Falling for the Hidden Folk Book 1

ELLA LARSON

Published by HRP Publishing

eBook ISBN: 978-82-93831-22-8

Paperback ISBN: 978-82-93831-23-5

Cover: Nirav Shah - @hobbysparrow_

Cover Typography: Rhea Fox

Glossary

Av – of
Bak – back
Bilde – picture
Brunost – brown cheese – a Norwegian speciality
Bålpan – campfire pan
Dal – Valley
De tre Bukkene Bruse – Three Billy Goats Gruff
Denne – this
Der – there
Du – you
Faen – fuck / the hell
Fast – tight
Flink – good
Først – first
Helvete – hell
Hva – what
Hysj – hush
Hytte – cabin
I morgen – tomorrow
Ja – yes
Jarl – Earl / Lord / Chief
Jenta – girl
Jævla – fucking
Kant – edge
Kjære – dear / dear one
Kuk – cock
La meg – let me

Meg – me
Naken – naked
Natt – night
Navn – name
Nei – no
Nydelig – gorgeous
Nå – now
Om – about
På ekte – really
Sjef – boss
Slutt – stop
Sånn – this / like this
Takk – thank you
Unnskyld – sorry
Vakt – Watch
Vei – way/ road
Å gir – to give
Å ha – to have
Å knulle – to fuck
Å komme – to come
Å se – to see
Å Snakke – to speak
Å sove – to sleep

Chapter 1

Cathy

"Smile," the golden-haired man says cheerily as he points the lens of my state-of-the-art camera in our direction.

I spread my lips in a wide smile, lacing my arms around the women at my sides. When was the last time we had had a photo of the four of us taken together? It must have been uni.

I grimace as the northern adonis lets my expensive piece of kit dangle from his fingers, but he sees my glare and hands it back with a shrug.

"Right, ladies, are you ready for your first trek? It will take us about three hours to ski to the lakeside where Stian..." He gestures at the large bearded man sat astride the snowmobile. It has a large trailer attached that contains not only our packs, but a couple of seats for those of us who are not so athletic. "Stian here will be waiting for us, and then after something to eat and a rest, we will continue for another couple of hours along the Nøkkmunnelva river to the base of Ilvarsfjell."

He claps his gloved hands together and rubs them eagerly, his grin growing even wider, which I didn't think was possible.

Sam and Izzy whoop with his contagious enthusiasm and begin strapping their feet into their long cross-country skis.

Tall, blonde Sam, who could pass as one of the local Norwegians herself, had been on all her school sports teams and is now training for her first athletics world cup. Her trainer wasn't happy about this impromptu trip until she told him about the skiing, at which point our itinerary had changed to include more of it...a lot more. She flips her long hair over her shoulder and raises an eyebrow at Izzy.

"You sure you can keep up? I have a program to stick to and I won't be slowing down for you."

The shorter woman glares up at her, thinly disguised venom in her words. "Just because I have the curves of a re-naissance painting, doesn't mean I'm not in good shape." She pulls her hat onto her darker blonde hair and tilts her head at the guide. "I can go all night long."

He grins and mutters something under his breath in Norwegian whilst eyeing Izzy up and down with obvious intent.

I need to diffuse the tension. It's been a while since we have been together and old habits are coming to the surface. "Come on you two — this is supposed to be a holiday, remember?"

I walk over to the snowmobile to put my camera away. I do enough sport to keep me trim, and whilst I am looking forward to skiing through this Nordic winter wonderland, I am more interested in the scenery.

My finger itches to press the shutter button on my new toy.

"Jeppe," I call over my shoulder to the ski guide. He bounds over, a pair of reflective sunglasses perched on his aquiline nose that are so slick, it looks like they have been spray-painted on.

"Yes, how can I help you? A problem with your skis per-haps?" he says in his sing-song accented English. It should have come across friendly, but I can tell by the way he glances back towards Sam and Izzy that he meant it to be condescending.

"No," I say tartly. I'd paid attention in the training les-son before we had been driven into the mountains and had even surprised myself with how quickly I had taken to the activity. I am a fast learner.

"I just think someone should stay with Lauren, at least until she is more comfortable in Stian's company. I'll join you after lunch on the tracks."

The lithe descendant of Vikings pulls a funny face, but then bows his head a little.

"As you wish. Enjoy the ride." Then he hollers something at the bearded man in Norwegian, gobbledegook to my ears, and raises two fingers to his black woollen hat in a cheeky salute.

"See you at the camp." The three skiers set off and Stian rises from the snowmobile with a grunt and a creak of leather and proceeds to pick my skis back up off the tracks where he had only moments before placed them.

"You don't have to babysit me, you know," Lauren mumbles, but I am glad when she laces her hand through mine. "At least not because of this, I hope." She lowers her hand to the small bump at her waistline, barely visible beneath her long-padded jacket.

I shake my head.

"No, I know you can take care of yourself, and bump. I just wanted to get some pictures done while the weather is nice. Besides, you know once those two are finished with lunch they will be on the go again."

She nods, tucks one of her black corkscrew curls behind her ear and raises an eyebrow, not quite believing me.

"Fine," I sigh, "I don't want you to be left alone all holiday... Had we known, we could have organised something different."

Lauren sighs and takes Stian's outstretched hand to help her into the back of the trailer. "I told you; I was not going to miss out on seeing Norway, and we are finally here after years of dreaming. Let's just enjoy it shall we, in whatever way we can."

I bite my lip, chastised. She had turned up at the airport, pregnant belly proceeding her, with no explanation. I knew from our time together at uni that Lauren would only talk when she was ready to. There is no sense in pushing.

"You, sit there, please." Stian's accent is thicker than Jeppe's and his English more broken, but I nod and sit on the opposite side to Lauren as he motions with his gloved hands, mumbling something about balancing the weight. I shoot Lauren a grin as the Norwegian lumbers back to his vehicle, the snow crunching under his feet. She claps her hands and smiles back as the engine roars to life, and then we are away, on our holiday of a lifetime!

CHAPTER 2

ÆRLEN

WE HEAR THE BUZZING of the engine far before the warning signals are tripped. It is a brash, intrusive noise that echoes around the valley.

My team is already out scouting, making sure any of our kind are aware of the night's events, the passing of the mountain trolls, when we hear it. The five of us freeze, pricking up our ears, guessing its distance.

"It's making its way through Dysterdal," Urug grunts at my side, breathing a plume of steam into the cold air, before turning to me. "What do you think?"

I pause, slowing my breath to think. Whoever it is, is in the neighbouring valley, a little too close for comfort. I cross my arms as the motor engine comes to an abrupt stop, leaving our ears ringing. It is then that I hear other noises and creep from the edge of the treeline.

Voices twitter in the winter sunlight, female voices. They are somewhere close but I strain my ears for another moment, sure I had heard something else. I tilt my head and the others follow suit. After a few moments, there it is again, more distant but there, the shush, shush, shush of skis on snow and the breathy pants of humans.

"Two parties," Torak snarls, his tail flicking angrily. I am about to put a hand on his arm to silence him but Fritha gets there first.

"It doesn't sound like many; perhaps we can misdirect them, turn them around before they come closer."

She looks up at me with her big blue eyes, a few golden strands of hair escaping her practical braid. It's always good to have a huldra in the Vakt in case of male humans — her song and good looks make it easy to cloud their minds and lure them back towards civilisation.

But I hear predominantly female voices and that piques my interest. I finally uncross my arms and turn to my team. "It could just be harmless day-trippers, out for a ski and a picnic."

It is a common occurrence when the humans have their religious festivals, but it's a long time from any of those, and at this time of year, the valley should be still.

"But considering tonight's crossing, I think we had better get a closer look. Find out if they intend to stay. Torak, Vedlun and Fritha…" Two trolls and the huldra step forwards. "You go and trail those skiers. You are the fastest and they are furthest away. Plus, they are more likely to have men in the group."

Truth be told, they are too far away to tell, but I know my countrymen quite well. I've never known a Norwegian male to pass up skiing on a day like this.

The threesome gives a quick nod and then disappears into the trees, the white coats and green-grey skin of Torak and Vedlun helping them blend into the snow-laden pines almost instantly. Fritha would know to stay back until she is needed, looking almost identical to the humans apart from her brown cow's tail that swishes as she moves.

"And us?" Urug crosses his arms, demanding an explanation as to why he hasn't been sent with the others.

Yes, he is strong and stealthy, but the sheer size of him does take a toll on his long-distance stamina. Not to mention his age. He must be twice as old as the rest of us. It's a wonder the Jarl allowed him to remain in the Valley Watch. I reach out and point down the valley, following the river until it widens and joins the frozen, snow-covered lake. He leans forward and squints, taking in the black snowmobile that shines in the sunlight.

Figures are moving around it, one setting up a camp and a *bålpan*, one settling itself on a stool, lifting its head to the sun as if in worship, and third heading for the treeline.

"You keep watch on that camp; I have a feeling that's where our skiers are heading, so we'll meet up with the others in the woods beyond."

He grunts, accepting his order. "And you, Ærlen, what will you be doing?"

I grind my teeth at his thinly veiled insult. As the oldest and strongest of the Vakt, he's always assumed he will be named Sjef of the valley patrol when my predecessor steps down, but he doesn't have the head for strategy. I point my finger at the lone figure disappearing into the pines. "I'll be tracking her."

Chapter 3

Cathy

I smile as I lower the viewfinder from my eye and check the last few shots.

The sun shining on the glittering snow is creating some absolutely stunning light effects as it refracts through the branches of the trees. I crouch in the snow and bite the top of my glove to take it off, unzipping my bag to reach for my macro lens.

I've always wanted to get a shot of a single snowflake, highlighting all its uniqueness, and the light is absolutely perfect. I swap the lenses and then rise, stalking to the branch of a tree. Its green needles shine in sharp contrast to the white dusting on top and as I bend forward, peering through the viewfinder, I gasp as I see the raw beauty of nature. I take a few shots at various angles and then sit back to inspect my work. They are perfect.

"Yes!" I punch the air with glee. I feel the flush of joy on my cheeks as I put the lens back in my bag and wonder what had taken me so long to ditch the corporate rat race that held me captive.

My joy falters as I remember. I'd stayed at that soul-sucking job with ridiculous job titles like 'Communications and Engagement Consultant', for years, getting promotion after promotion, taking on more stress and more responsibilities, because of him. I clench my teeth as his name hisses from my lips. "Ed."

We'd started at the firm together, first teammates and then rivals for the promotions, but he was always one step ahead of me. Eventually our animosity came to a crashing halt as we'd ended up having too much to drink, followed by an argument, followed by — I blush as the memories hit me — the hottest angry sex I'd ever had. Then we'd fallen into the routine of shacking up every time we'd had a bad day and needed to get all the pent-up energy out.

Somewhere along the line that had calmed down and he'd actually introduced me to his family and other friends. We became the power couple of Rowland Enterprises, the ones to watch. That was until, of course, Mr Rowland, CEO, had invited us all to dinner at his private estate, where we met the stunning heiress to his fortune, Miss Eliza Rowland.

I should have known.

The minute he laid eyes on her, he dropped my hand and whipped out that oh-so-charming smile I hadn't seen in years.

I sigh and pull on my gloves again, making sure the camera bag is zipped up tight. I shake my head to banish the memories of him growing distant, of walking in on them together and then my very embarrassing drunken beratement of them in front of my boss.

Needless to say, I no longer work at Rowland Enterprises and I am no longer with Ed.

"Fucking prick," I spit as I step back towards the camp.

My stomach growls and I know my sudden bad mood is exacerbated by that, but the thought of him, now engaged to Miss Eliza Rowland and being made a partner, makes my blood boil.

I close my eyes and take a deep breath in through my nose before pushing the air out of my mouth through rounded lips. I need to centre myself. I am not going to let him ruin this perfect holiday and the start to my new career. The pictures I take here will make up my new portfolio.

I repeat the breathing for a few more cycles, feeling the cold brush against the inside of my nostrils and the vapour of my breath kiss my cheeks before rising into the brilliant blue sky.

Finally, I open my eyes and see a footprint. At first, my brain can't comprehend what I am staring at. It's just an animal track, surely. My heart leaps at the thought of catching a deer or even something larger like a moose or wolf (even if that does send a prickle of fear down my spine), but then as I look through my camera, pressing down on the shutter button, I realise it can't be.

There, in the snow before my very eyes, is a trail of prints, each one looking like a squashed and distorted 8 shape, like a boot print, only there were no familiar brand markings and it is much, much bigger than a human's print.

I swallow, racking my brain to remember if they have abominable snowmen sightings here in Norway, or was that Nepal, when a movement up ahead makes me look up and zoom in on the trees about fifty metres away.

The tracks lead that way, and whatever it is, is still there, watching me. With my naked eye, I make out a huge, hulking shape hugging the tree trunk, trying to vanish into the shadows of its branches.

Holy shit...what if it is a bear? I know they have those here, even if they should all be hibernating at this time of year. All the more reason for me to get the fuck out of here. If I had stumbled across a sleepy, no doubt angry bear, I would have been in ribbons before I knew it, yet something stops me. I know it's crazy, but I pause and raise my camera to my eye for the last time.

I zoom into the shape as much as I can, still not able to see it clearly. Suddenly the creature moves, so I press my finger down, and with a yelp and the most colourful vocabulary in the English language, I turn on my heel and run.

Chapter 4

Cathy

I arrive back at the camp, my cheeks hot and my lungs burning from running as fast as I can through thick snow drifts. I look over my shoulder as I fly through the final few trees before the clearing to check nothing is following me and crash straight into Jeppe.

"Cathy!" he coos, arms outstretched and that slimy smile all over his face "What has you running into my arms in such a panic?"

He winks at me as I push him away, the wool of his sweater slightly damp from his exertions. Izzy glares at me but I don't take any notice. She can have this smarmy charmer with pleasure.

"There was something big, in the trees," I blurt out, shaking my head and trying to get my breath back as he leads me behind the others skiers out into the open. "I couldn't see what it was."

The two Norwegians look at each other and the gruff, bearded Stian takes a step towards me. "Was it a wolf, do you think? Strange for them to be out in the day, but possible."

I shake my head as the other girls swing their heads between me and the guides, alarm making their eyes wide.

"No," I stammer. "It was too big and looked like it was stood up against a tree. I thought a bear..."

Suddenly the seriousness in Stian's face melts away and he smiles, shaking his head.

"No, no bears. They sleep now."

And that's it, as if the matter is over. I stamp my foot on the snow.

"But I saw something, I know I did." I am about to raise my camera to show them when Jeppe places his hands on my upper arms, pinning them in place, and guides me to a stool, pushing me down onto it.

"Perhaps you saw one of the famous Norwegian trolls," he says with a twinkle in his eye as he walks over to the small table set up by the fire. Isobelle laughs, a high-pitched tinkling that sounds just a bit too put-on.

"What, like those ugly little statues they have in all the gift shops, with big noses, bigger hair and tails? They don't look so frightening." Lauren laughs, shaking her head.

"Oh, come on," Sam scoffs haughtily, flipping her poker-straight hair out of her face with a twist of her swanlike neck. "Trolls aren't real."

Stian, who is busy squeezing some pink, grainy looking stuff out of a tube and onto a slice of bread — *kaviar*, apparently — raises a finger.

"Some believed trolls were as big as mountains; others, that they were more like us, but believe in them they did. Norge is a wild land, with many remote and unreached places. Maybe all the trolls and other creatures are just hiding."

A silence falls, broken only by the crackling of the fire. Samantha's eyebrows rise high with incredulity. Isobelle stares at Jeppe for his reaction and as a shiver creeps up my spine, I notice Lauren pale.

"Other creatures?" she breathes, a tremble in her voice.

Suddenly Jeppe claps his hands and laughs.

"Stian is only being funny, and even if they did exist, or even if it was a bear..." He walks over to the snowmobile and pulls out a rifle. "We have guns. So, you are all perfectly safe, ladies." He puts the gun back down, strapping it into place, and comes back to the table, picking up a cheese slicer and brandishing it over a block of what looked like dynamite. "Now, who wants *brunost*?"

I raise my hand as my stomach growls. Perhaps I'm just hungry and my imagination had been playing tricks on me. I let the conversation wash over me as I eat. The strange brown cheese, sweet, almost like caramel, sticks to the roof of my mouth a bit, but is soon washed down with strong, steaming coffee. Jeppe passes me another slice, this time with some sort of cheese from a tube decorating the bread in a wavy pattern. What is the obsession with food in tubes? Half of our supplies consist of them.

I eat this one more gingerly, not failing to notice how Lauren takes one sniff and sets the slice back on the table with a grimace.

"Can I look at your photos, Cathy?" she asks, reaching for my camera. Seeing as my mouth is glued together by the sticky cheese paste, I nod, but lean closer to her stool to peer over her shoulder. Her comments and compliments make me smile with pride as she flicks through them. When we come to the end of the reel, she pauses, the corners of her mouth turning down in a frown.

"What's this one?"

I wipe my hands on my trouser legs and take the camera from her, peering into the digital screen. "Oh, this is the animal I thought I saw."

We look down at it and sure enough, there up against a tree, though partly hidden by branches, is a huge dark shape.

"Can you zoom in any more? I can't make it out." I pull the camera closer to me and fiddle with the buttons. Though I had zoomed in with the lens when I took the picture, I might be able to see more clearly on here; either that, or the image would become so distorted I would be none the wiser.

"Well?"

She tries to lean in to see more, but I pull the camera away, hoping my voice doesn't sound too shaky when I speak. "Nothing, it just gets blurry the more you zoom in."

She sits back, seemingly mollified, but I stare down at the photo one more time, the pit dropping out of my stomach as a face stares back at me, eyes glittering between the branches. Whatever I had seen was definitely not a bear and is definitely still out there.

CHAPTER 5

ÆRLEN

I was seen.

By the Gods, this was the worst thing that could have happened. The woman with the delicious scent that wafted through the trees had seen me, and what's more, in the split second before she ran, her camera had been pointed straight at me.

I curse myself as I follow her, more discreetly this time, back to her camp where I find the others waiting, hidden but watching.

"What kept you?" Urug growls. "I've been freezing my bollocks off sat here watching these two."

I grunt a noncommittal response. There is no way I was going to tell my team how much I have just fucked up. I would be kicked off the *Vakt* for sure, or at the very least be demoted, handing my position to Torak or, the Gods forbid, Urug, and my hopes of becoming village leader with it. I have to get that camera back.

"Did you learn anything?" I whisper hurriedly.

"No," he growls. "Only, this woman is with child and this man eats too much herring. Can smell his breath from here. No news, so let's go."

I brush off his comment and turn to the team of three who had been following the skiers.

"You three? News? Did you find out what they were up to?"

Torak snorts. "You mean apart from the blatant pre-mating of two of them? Yes, we know where they are going." He crosses his arms and motions with his head up towards the mountain.

"They will ski to the cabin on the border of Heimli, you know, the one that has all those loud parties at Juletid and Sommernatt."

I nod grimly. I knew it.

The luxury cabin is located right at the entrance to our valley, and is always a cause for extra Vakt when its residents come for high days and holidays, with their loud music, drink and, more often than not, nudity as the partygoers rut like animals.

In a way it is refreshing, reminding me of the old times before the robed men with their crosses turned this country from the old Gods and made intimate pleasure sin. Often, on Vakt, I watch, not the whole thing, but enough to make me envious of these small weak men who have enough money to make a whole horde of women fall at their feet. They don't deserve it, not when I see the way they treat these women at their parties, like objects, toys. I sigh, reprimanding myself — surely, they are not all like that — and bring myself back to the present.

"Hmm, we will need to watch them further. *Nattvakt,* I'm afraid."

A groan rises from my team at the prospect of the night watch, but there is no way we can let this group out of our sight, especially not when the stone trolls are on the move.

I peer back towards their makeshift camp. The men are starting to pack up, the female skiers jumping to their feet, keen to follow the river up to the *hytte.* The pretty brunette, I can see her hair now she has removed her hat, is still sat bent over her camera. I watch in horror as her eyes widen, her hands shake and she snatches it away from the pregnant woman who is trying to see.

I swallow, a stone-like lump suddenly in my throat. My tail swishes nervously as I realise she had not only seen me, but she does indeed have my likeness in that instrument, and she knows what I am. I stand and point up the valley to my comrades.

"Torak, Vedlun and Fritha — keep to your targets. Urug, continue to trail the mother."

He grumbles but stalks off to carry out his duty.

"Looks like you'll be with us, *Sjef*." Fritha tilts her head in the direction of the camp. Everyone is moving now and the brown-haired beauty I have been trailing is busy packing her camera into her backpack and preparing to ski. I glower. This would make things more difficult, surrounded by my teammates. I have to destroy that camera somehow without them seeing. I nod and slink into the treeline behind the others as the skiers begin to move.

Although they wear skis and move at a brisk pace, it is no problem for us to keep up, honed by years of running through the mountains, but as the minutes pass, I realise my target is slower than the others. Her breath catches more often, and her cheeks are red. She is not used to this.

A sudden thought strikes me. If she falls behind enough, especially once they leave the open space by the river, I may just be able to intercept her and solve my little problem. The corners of my mouth rise, the tips of my fangs catching the frosty air as I smile. All I have to do is sit back and bide my time.

CHAPTER 6

CATHY

MY MOOD LIFTS AS I ski alongside the river, the low sun making sparkles on the small patches of water visible through the blue ice. The sound of running water also calms me. I've always loved being by water.

Occasionally I stop to snap a picture of two of the landscape and my fellow skiers up ahead for posterity's sake, but it is soon made clear that they are getting tired of waiting for me. We ski a bit, me pushing myself as hard as I can, but still lagging behind, and they shoot off ahead, leaving clear tracks for me to follow. When I lose sight of them as we turn back into the forest, I panic, but a few minutes more skiing and I find them waiting for me as I round a bend.

"Do try to keep up, Cathy," Izzy says nonchalantly, drinking from her water bottle in the most seductive way possible, making sure Jeppe is watching. She is flushed pink like me, but she won't admit she is tired even if she is. As always, she has to prove she can keep up with Sam, that her size won't stop her from doing anything the beautiful athlete can. Jeppe smirks and adjusts the waistband of his trousers as a drip of water runs down Izzy's chin.

Urgh, I wish they would just get it over with and fuck tonight; all this flirting is making me want to vomit.

Sam simply raises an elegant but unimpressed eyebrow.

I skid to a stop and reach for my own water bottle, the sharp coolness of its contents splashing down my front as

I gulp messily, spluttering at the unfairness that they are already moving off again.

Bastards. Weren't tour guides supposed to go at the pace of the slowest in the group?

Jeppe calls over his shoulder to me. "We're on the last stretch now. About one kilometre to go, before we hit the ascent."

"Ascent?" I cry. I am only just managing to ski flat, let alone uphill.

"You'll see the cabin once we clear these last trees, and then you are home and dry. Just follow our tracks."

And then they are off, leaving me open-mouthed with astonishment. It is starting to get dark despite the early hour, and hadn't Jeppe said night was when the wolves come out? I slam my water bottle back into my bag and swing it onto my back. I will be writing a very strongly worded letter of complaint to the tour company when I get back home.

Chapter 7

Ærlen

It is now or never. The others have left her behind, and in the next ten minutes or so, she will be out of the treeline. Torak, Fritha and Vedlun had rolled their eyes at the slow member of the group and while the guide's disgraceful behaviour makes me growl, concerned for the woman's safety, it is to my advantage.

I stalk closer, close enough to hear her mumbling angrily under her strained breath as she pushes herself onwards. She is tiring now, unused to so much prolonged exercise, another factor that will aid my mission. I've been watching her every time she stops to take a photo, and know that her camera sits right at the top of her bag.

If I am quick, I can run past and snatch it before she notices anything. I bend myself lower into a huddled crouch, keeping pace with her and preparing to dash behind her. I take a deep, steadying breath and propel myself forward.

It would have worked, should have worked, but at the very moment I spring from my hiding place, she lets out a cry of frustration, tears in her eyes, and turns to fetch her water bottle tucked into the side pocket of her bag, giving her a full-frontal view of me running towards her.

Her eyes widen so much, I can see the sparkling green of them, but there is no time to admire them. Her mouth is opening, her breath drawing in, ready to let out as an ear-splitting scream. So, I dive onto her, slapping my hand across her dainty little mouth as I fall on top of her, pressing her into the snow.

CHAPTER 8

CATHY

I KICK AND TRY to scream but the sheer weight of this thing, this creature, is pinning me down into the snow. My legs are bent at awkward angles due to the long, thin skis on my feet, but I still writhe and manage to hit his back with them a couple of times.

He grunts what sounded like "ow" and then placing a hand behind my head to protect it, he gives it a sharp jolt.

"*Hysj!*" he hisses into my ear. Hush? Had this thing that had barrelled me over just told me to hush?

I stop moving, stop trying to scream as all the fight goes out of me and I look up. My eyes widen as they meet the same large black ones that had stared out of my camera at me, only this time, I can see all of its face.

A mass of brown hair, almost like reeds, frame a male face. It sticks up at all angles, easy to mistake for brush or leaves. He is so close that some of it tickles my cheeks and I'm surprised by how soft it is.

But my fear has not abated quite yet. Only an inch from my nose is a face, a green face, with a more prominent than usual nose and thick, darker green lips curled in a snarl, exposing two white fangs.

I yelp instinctively and one of my skis slaps him across the back of his legs. He hisses, as if forcing himself not to roar, and mutters, "*Slutt!*"

My jaw drops. What the fuck did he just call me? He must see the offence in my eyes as he gives his own a hefty roll and he speaks again. "*Stopp!*"

A movement catches my eye. Over the top of his head, where my ski is hovering, an appendage snaps up and wraps its tufted tip around the width of it, holding it up and away from his body. A tail. This thing...this green man has a tail.

I squirm, not sure where I'm trying to get to, when I become aware of the sheer size of him, the weight and rigidity of him as his body presses mine into the snow. His chest is slightly raised, allowing me to see the bulk of hidden muscles, before tapering down where our bellies meet. He seems to be using more force to keep me still by pressing down with his large quads and his pelvis, pushing into me so hard I feel the hefty bulge of his cock grinding between my legs.

Heat rises to my cheeks. Fuck. The very thought sends signals of want down my spine and to my horror, my own body responds to his, heating and clenching, forcing my own pelvis to squirm under his. I whimper against the enormous hand covering my mouth and see something soften in those black eyes. The green man raises a finger to his lips and seems to ask this time.

"*Hysj?*"

He wants me to be quiet? Well, if that means getting released from this highly compromising situation, then I can be quiet.

I nod, feeling my lips brush against the roughness of his palm, and he very slowly withdraws his hand. We stay like that a few moments longer, staring at one another, my heart pounding against his chest, before he crawls back up into a kneeling position between my legs and very gently unclips my skis.

I groan with relief as the deft flicks of his fingers on my boots allow my legs to return to a more natural position and he shoots me a look, as if preparing to leap on me again. I quickly raise a finger to my lips.

"Hush." I whisper. "See, I'm quiet."

I have no idea whether this thing can understand me. What is he?

My own brain laughs as it makes the connection between the small caricature-like figures in the tourist gift shops and the hulking male specimen before me.

He is a troll. A real live troll. I swallow and scoot a little further away, shaking as the snow I had rolled in begins to melt with the heat of my body.

"What do you want?" I ask, my lips trembling as my eyes roam over his body to the hard bulk that had pressed in between my legs only moments before. I can see something long and hard straining against the fabric of his trousers.

Does he have a hard on...or is that just how big it is? I snap my eyes to his face. His lips curve up slightly, as if trying not to smile. Shit, he'd seen where I was looking, had seen my raised eyebrow.

I repeat my question hastily, hoping he doesn't want what I'd made perfectly clear I think he does. To my relief, he shakes his head and points at my bag.

"You want my bag?" I say incredulously. Is this some kind of troll stand-and-deliver highwayman? Is he mugging me? A small rumble comes from this throat that sounds like frustration, but it sends goosepimples down my arms. He snatches my bag and begins to unzip it.

I jump to action, trying to grab it from him, but he is too strong and simply swats me away as if I am a fly. Then he pulls out my camera.

My belly fills with ice as he raises it above his head next to the pine beside us, ready to smash.

"No!" I shout, breaking our pact to be quiet, but it stills his hand as he whirls around to face me, hissing his order again.

"*Hysj*!"

I stand and square up to him, aware that he towers over me but I can't let him smash my camera. It's my livelihood, the only thing keeping me from slipping back into the depression the shitshow of my redundancy had left me in for months.

"Don't smash my camera..." I reach out and place a gloved hand on his forearm. "Please."

My touch stills him, and he looks down at my hand, tiny against his bulk. His lips move as if he's searching for words and then he speaks, a deep bass rumble that reverberates through his arm and right through me.

"*Du har bilde av meg.*"

I shake my head, wishing I had spent just a bit more time studying some Norwegian.

"I'm sorry, I don't understand. Do you speak English?" I cringe at the question. I'd always tried to learn the language of the country I was visiting, not wanting to appear stupid, but this trip had been so last minute. He sighs and I see his eyes flicking as he thinks. He raises a hand and points to his chest.

"I..." His accent is thick and his voice uncertain as he wraps his mouth around the unfamiliar words. "I...am in *kamera.*"

He is in the camera? Then it hits me. He knows I have a picture of him and obviously doesn't want anyone to see it. I nod.

"Ok, alright, I'll delete it," I hold out my hand for the DSLR and nod encouragingly. "Let me show you."

I don't know if he understands all the words but he sighs and lowers his hand, placing the equipment in mine. I move slowly, turning my back to him and looking up over my shoulder as I switch it on.

"See..." I say as I scroll through the photos I had taken that afternoon. "Just pictures of the lake, really."

He steps closer to see, but the movement presses his chest into my back and my senses go into overdrive. Every inch of my skin tingles and my nose is filled with the scent of pine, a hint of woodsmoke and something undeniably masculine and musky. My throat goes dry as I become innately aware of every breath he takes. Suddenly, he jabs at the screen with a large finger, at least twice the size of a normal man's.

"*Der.*"

There. It is the picture of him, blurred in the treeline but the humanoid shape is clear.

"I'll delete it." I repeat, pressing the buttons slowly so he can watch. When it's gone, I feel him release a breath and for a split second he sags into me with relief. Then he pats my shoulder, a gesture that makes my breath hitch, and he steps away from me smiling.

"*Takk.*" Thank you.

I nod and bend down to put my camera away again. It's almost dark now, so I find my headlamp and put it on. When I turn to face him, he hisses and I hurriedly switch it to a lower setting.

"Sorry, sorry."

Evidently, trolls can see in the dark. He watches as I put my skis back on and look around, now completely disorientated. He approaches, hands held up like I am an animal about to shy. Then with his hands on my upper arms, he turns me around and points over my shoulder.

In the dim light, I can see the track leading out of the trees and if I look higher, I see the lights of the cabin twinkling welcomingly.

"*Denne veien,*" he says in my ear, his hot breath caressing my chilled cheek. I look back up at him, and realise our faces are only inches apart.

I feel a pull inside me, one that I haven't felt in such a long time, the terrifying excitement before a first kiss. But that was insane, I couldn't possibly want to kiss a troll, could I? I mean, he has fangs. But as he rises to his full height, putting distance between us, I am surprised to find myself somewhat disappointed.

For the third time, he raises a finger to his lips.

"You not speak of me." It's half a question, half an order.

I shake my head. There is no way I am ever going to speak to anyone about this...encounter. They would think I'd snapped.

"No, I won't tell." I lace my hands through the ski pole handles, ready to leave, but pause. "Goodbye...um...I'm sorry, I don't know your name?"

His brow crinkles as he thinks about what I'd said. Then he cocks his lips up into a crooked side smile and places a hand on his chest.

"*Mitt navn er Ærlen.*" Then in his accented English, which he seems to be digging from some deep memory, asks, "What is your name?"

I smile and place hand on my own chest.

"My name is Cathy."

He repeats, pronouncing the 'th' as a hard 't' sound.

"Catty?" He bunches his hand into a claw shape and meows at me questioningly. I can't help but laugh.

"Cathy," I repeat, putting the emphasis on the 'th' by making my tongue visible between my teeth. He copies my action and I am struck by the long, thin point of a blue tongue.

"Cathy." His low rumble makes my legs feel like they have turned to melted butter.

"It's short for Catherine," I burble, not quite sure what else to say.

Ærlen points up the hill, as if to remind me where I was going.

"*Takk* Cathy," he says in a final whisper before turning and disappearing into the dark trees.

CHAPTER 9

ÆRLEN

WELL, THAT DIDN'T EXACTLY go as planned.

Could my fuck ups get any greater today? First, I'd allowed myself to get captured on camera, then I had actually been seen and interacted with one of these humans...not only that, but now I couldn't stop thinking about her.

Sure, my nerves had been pounding as I'd barrelled into her to shut her up, but then as she softened underneath me, I was aware of all she was: the determined soul that shone out from those emerald-green eyes; the scent of her, vanilla and something floral; and then, oh Gods, the way her curves moulded into my own body.

I groan as my cock jumps to attention at the thought. I will have to do something about that later, but now is not the time.

I follow her at a safe distance through the woods, watching as she makes her slow way up to the cabin where all the others had arrived long before. My heart swells with pride as I see her shout at them for leaving her but thankfully, she keeps her promise and says nothing of me.

"Cathy," I breathe, placing my tongue between my teeth the way she had done, showing just the tip, a small pink bud that I had wanted to flick with my own.

"What did you say?" Vedlun whispers at my side, shifting into a better position on the snow drift we are hidden behind.

"Oh, um, nothing," I mumble, cursing my slip. I turn my eyes back to the *hytte* where the four women are streaming from the door wrapped in towels, heading for the hot tub, squealing as the cold attacks their bare flesh.

"Here we go." Torak leans forward to get a closer view. We all do; it has been a long time since we have seen almost naked women, having long exhausted the limited choices left to us in Heimli. Those not related to us have chosen other mates, and now here we were, the last generation, with no way to carry on our lineage.

I swallow as I watch Cathy remove her towel and walk up the steps, my mouth suddenly dry and my cock stiffening with every movement she makes. Her skin is smooth and creamy, at odds with the rich chocolate of her hair which is now tied up on top of her head, showing the long, graceful curve of her neck. Her shoulders are slender and the straps of her bathing suit hardly seem enough to hold up the plump tits that sit above the slim waist that I want to wrap my hands around. Just before she slips into the water she turns and I get a full-on view of her ass: round, and sticking out from that waist like a shelf. I muffle another groan as I think how much I want to grab each cheek and... But my attention is distracted as the human men block my view. One is wearing only bathing shorts, holding a tray of champagne glasses, but the other is fully dressed in his snowmobile gear.

I can't hear what is said but the large bearded man soon heads off, starts the engine of the vehicle and disappears down the mountain.

"Do you think we need to follow him?" Fritha hisses in my ear, ready to move. Men are her speciality. I turn my head in his direction, watching the red lights and the back of his vehicle disappear into the trees.

"No. Looks like he is going back to the village. That's one less for us to worry about."

We are quiet for a time as we watch the party. The pregnant female with the dark skin sits on the side, only her feet in the bubbling pool, drinking a soda instead of the champagne the blonde man has passed around.

I keep my eyes trained on Cathy. She takes it and sips gingerly, trying to scooch away from the man as he forces himself into the hot tub, sending a wave of water sploshing over the side.

I feel a rumble grow in my chest as he moves to put his arm around Cathy and the woman on his other side, jealousy getting the better of me. Now that I had touched her, spoken to her, smelt her, she was imprinted on my brain...

I grimace and nod curtly as she gives the jock a stern look and moves away from him to the other side of the pool, making it very clear she is unimpressed with his advances.

That's *my* woman. I shake my head at myself. My woman? I had only talked to the woman once, what right did I have over her? But the more I watch her, the more I know: if she isn't my mate, then I will have none other. I want her.

I glance over at the faces of my team. Fritha looks bored, Torak is grumbling that he can't see anything and Vedlun has wandered further up the mountain to watch for the stone trolls starting their crossing.

Urug, normally the one to make crude jokes or gestures when we had to watch the human fornication parties, is strangely silent, his eyes trained on the mother-to-be. I furrow my brow and am about to ask if he has seen something he likes, when we all feel it.

Deep down in the earth, in the very bedrock of the mountains, something rumbles. I glance at the sky, and by now the moon is full and round, shining with an intense brilliance on the snow-covered landscape. The stone trolls are waking up.

Chapter 10

Cathy

We don't stay too long in the hot tub.

It's not fair on Lauren who can't come in and the more Jeppe pours into our glasses, the more I want a protective layer of clothing between us. I hadn't liked the greedy sheen in his eyes when he had clambered in, stretching an arm around Izzy and, to my horror, me.

The idea of him touching me, like he had a right to, makes my flesh crawl, unlike the thought of the hulking green troll who had made it tingle.

I shake my head at my foolishness, actually catching myself wondering if he was out there, watching. If he was, what would he think of me in a bikini? My cheeks flush at the thought. Still, I spend a little more time drying myself off as I leave the hot tub, not even wrapping my towel around me as I walk back inside...just in case.

I hurry back into my clothes now, aware of the gorgeous full moon outside that I simply have to capture.

I turn to Jeppe as he emerges from his room, towelling off his golden hair.

"Do you think we will see the lights tonight?"

He reaches for his phone and mumbles to himself as he checks stats and then looks up at me, beaming.

"Yes, I should think so, and not too long from now. So, get bundled up ladies, grab a beer and let's head outside for Norway's greatest natural show."

I roll my eyes. He is such a showman that it makes me cringe. Like those influencers who are just too happy all the time.

I sigh. Maybe I am just getting old and bitter with my thirties on the horizon. There are so many things I had hoped to do by now, like a marriage, a house, a career and thinking about kids, but nope.

Here I was on a girl's holiday, single and about to embark on a new and very uncertain future.

I nod at Jeppe, still not forgiving him for leaving me in the wilderness to get attacked by a troll, and grab my snow pants, jacket, hat, scarf and gloves. The others are in similar states of dress, Izzy clinking beer bottles with Jeppe and taking selfies, while Sam places a hand on Lauren's bump and they both smile, in a shy but familiar way. I snatch up my camera bag as we troop out the door back into the cold, noticing Jeppe switching off the lights as we go. He smiles at me and hands me a bottle of beer.

"I want you to get the best photos, so there will be no interference from man-made lights." He points at the sky. "Besides, we hardly need them with this moon."

We start to walk a little way from the cabin to where a circle of wooden benches is covered with furs around an unlit firepit, but before we can get there, dark shapes move from the treeline and our path is blocked.

Huge, looming figures crunch over the snow towards us, hair sticking up wildly, white teeth glittering in the moonlight, their tails swishing. Trolls!

Izzy screams and hides behind Jeppe who stops and stares at them open-mouthed.

Sam puts herself before Lauren, whose eyes are trained on the largest of them all, the one with no hair at all, her brows furrowed.

I realise I am wearing the same confused expression as I make eye contact with Ærlen. What the hell?

Had he liked what he had seen so much he had told his friends to come along for rape and pillage? Wasn't that what trolls and Vikings were famous for?

Jeppe grabs Izzy's arm and is about to run back to the *hytte* when a deep voice booms in the clearing.

"*Halt!*" My knees weaken when I realise that order had come from Ærlen. He rattles off something quickly in what I assume to be Norwegian, although it has a difference cadence to it, and the others move, surrounding us.

"You must *kom*. Not safe here." He looks at me imploringly, a deep panic written across his face. I shake my head.

"Why? Why isn't it safe?" Jeppe seems to have found his backbone and steps forward, pointing a finger at the evident leader of this pack of otherworldly creatures. Then he switches back to Norwegian to deliver what I can only assume to be a string of insults. "*Hva i helvete snakker du om, du jaevla fettkjerring?*"

I don't understand the words but from the tone of his voice, it can't have been anything nice. Ærlen takes a step towards me. I am rooted to the spot, unable to move as his scent washes over me.

"The stone trolls move. They *kom nå*. Will *smasj hytta*, will make snow fall down mountain. Must leave *nå*."

Sam grabs my arm, her grip iron, and pulls me back into their protective huddle.

"What the fuck are you talking about? There are no stone trolls..." But the words die on her lips as she takes in the band before her. If these trolls exist, then surely the other ones do, too?

As if to further disprove her thinking, the ground beneath our feet rumbles. Ærlen looks back over his shoulder and then to me, holding out his huge green hand, pleading.

"You stay, you die. *Kom*...please."

My heart is thundering in my ribcage. Is this a trick? But with every second that ticks by, the rumbling under our feet gets stronger, the trees shake and the snow begins to fall from their branches. I can't tear my eyes away from Ærlen's, scanning them for the truth, but I find only fear and insistence there.

A movement to my left breaks the spell. Lauren steps out from behind Sam and towards the enormous bald troll, reaching up a shaking hand and placing it on his chest. What is she doing? She puts her other hand on her belly protectively and looks up at him with wide eyes.

"Can you save us both?"

The troll grunts and before I can blink, he sweeps Lauren up in his arms as if she weighs nothing and runs back into the treeline. Well, if she is putting her unborn child's life in a troll's hands, then I should trust the pull inside me and take Ærlen's. As I do, he swings me up onto his back piggyback style and motions for the other trolls to do the same.

"Man must run. Cannot carry him."

I feel his words vibrate through his body and into me. Jeppe looks at me on Ærlen's back and Sam clambering onto another's, and takes a step back, shaking his head. Izzy is stuck in the middle, unsure what to do.

"Izzy, come on!" I shout as the ground begins to buck now, and even Ærlen is struggling to keep his footing. She looks back at Jeppe, who snarls, "You crazy bitches!" and runs back to the side of the cabin, abandoning us to the troll and the impending avalanche as he jumps onto a spare snowmobile and vanishes down the hillside.

A figure runs after him, a woman... What is she doing here? But Ærlen shouts after her in his language and she gives off the chase. He shouts again to another troll to pick Izzy up with ease despite her cries of objection and as soon as she has been slung over his shoulder, runs.

CHAPTER 11

ÆRLEN

I RUN AS FAST as I can, the earth juddering under my feet, the snow already sliding. What an idiot I had been. I should have got them out sooner but I had been distracted by watching them, watching *her* in the hot tub.

There are panicked breaths in my ear and I feel her little hands clasped around my neck as she tries to hold on. Her thighs are clenching around my waist and I give them a squeeze of encouragement.

I will not let any harm come to her, but first we have to get off this side of the mountain. Each step I take makes her frame bounce away from me and then as I land, her spread legs slam into my back, forcing sweet whimpers from her lips.

For a split second I wonder what it would feel like, sound like, if our naked flesh was slamming together like that as I fuck her. Then to my surprise, I realise she must be thinking along the same lines, as the smell of her arousal wafts up to my nostrils.

No! Now is really not the time!

Urug has set the path, running down into the valley and then up the opposing slope to the entrance to the Dal. We have to hurry; the moment those stone trolls walk across the mountain, they will dislodge the snow-capped peak, causing an avalanche of such magnitude its destruction and debris will swamp the whole region.

"Hold meg fast," I say, not sure what the word for 'tight' is in English, but she responds to my command by instinct

as I propel myself up the slope and gravity attempts to rip her from my back.

Although she is light, the strain of her extra weight and my panicked exertion is making my lungs burn, but I can't give up. If I stop now, both me and Cathy will be buried under the snow. I power on, using her heartbeat pounding against my back to set my pace.

We are out of the treeline now and it's only a final climb to the ledge where my team and their charges are waiting.

Fritha calls out to encourage me, and Torak and Vedlun, both casting fearful glances over my shoulder at the other slope, are bent down, hands outstretched to pull me up. As I leap, the world rocks and I almost don't grasp the splintered rocky edge. Cathy screams and holds on tighter, clawing her way up my body to the outstretched hands.

I let her step up on my shoulders as I hang there, my arms aching as the light from the full moon dims. When my brethren pull me up over the ledge, I turn and watch as a house-sized stone troll crests the ridge.

Chapter 12

Cathy

Holy shit!

Not only had my pussy just been pounded into the middle of next week as we had run for our lives, leaving me in a strange sense of survivalist's arousal, I was now staring up at a thing from nightmares.

An enormous figure is climbing over the top of the mountain we had been on only moments ago, its massive, stone like-hands crushing the snow like icing sugar. Illuminated perfectly in the full moon, I see that he is something of legend, a literal man made of the mountain, with trees and moss growing from his shoulders, his thighs, which are now gripping the mountain ridge as he hauls himself over.

I *have* to get a picture of this. Just think, if I was the photographer to capture a stone troll...my career would be set. My hands move instinctively and I take the cap off the lens and start to shoot.

I snap the monster in various stages as he climbs over the mountain, hauls himself to his full height, and then, to the horror of all watching, walks down the slope in a sea of tumbling snow towards the cabin.

The camera falls from my face and I watch, dumbstruck, as the building we had been staying in is swamped by snow that moves so fast it looks like a flash flood. Only the pointed tip of it is visible.

I hear a choked gasp from one of the girls, Izzy maybe, as the stone troll blindly sets his foot on what remains, causing an explosion of timber and other manmade objects that are swept away in the deluge. But there is no time to process what has just happened as the avalanche spreads towards us, climbing up the hillside we have just climbed, swallowing trees whole.

"Bak! Bak fra kanten! Nå!" Ærlen picks himself up from the rocky outcrop and stands, arms outspread as if to herd us towards the rock at our backs, away from the edge. As the roaring of the world fills my ears, I have no issue following his orders, and scuttle back. He takes a step towards me, as if to protect me, but then his eyes settle on the camera in my hand and his eyes turn dark.

He storms towards me and I turn, shoving my gear back in my bag, walking as far along the ledge as I can.

"No *foto*!" he bellows over the crash of destruction. *"Gi meg kameraen!"*

I don't know his words but his intentions are clear as he reaches for my camera bag.

"NO!" I scream. "It's all I have!"

His lips bare to expose his white, fanged teeth and if it hadn't been for the noise, I know I would have heard him growl.

I stamp my foot and shake my head. Who does he think he is? He lunges to try and swipe my gear, but mid-flight, the expression in his eyes changes from anger to panic as they flick upwards to see a river of snow and rock heading straight for us.

My heart stops as I follow his gaze and my knees give way, but suddenly he is there, not threatening me, but arched over me, protecting me as the rubble-strewn snow streams past, cutting us from the rest of the group.

As the world rushes by in deadly chaos, I look up, our eyes meet and time seems to slow. He stands, towering over me, his hands either side of my head, his body pressed against mine. His scent overwhelms me, the pine, woodsmoke and musk filling the enclosed space until I am not breathing air any more. I am breathing him.

My breath falters as I realise that just like air, this is something I cannot live without now that it has infiltrated every cell of my being. Something has changed and something in my chest tugs, as if a cord binds me to him. It feels frightening and wonderful all at the same time.

I forget the crashing, the boom of rocks falling, and hear only our laboured pants turn from frightened, to confused, to something else. His eyes flick down to my lips which are parted as I gasp for air and I crane my head upwards instinctively.

My whole body is trembling now and while logic tells me it is from the adrenaline of a near-death experience, I know it is from want. There is a final rumble, and Ærlen presses himself into me further, protecting me, but it forces a choked gasp from me as his pelvis grinds into mine.

He is hard and knowing his beating heart against my ear is also due to desire, I feel my core heat and then clench. His hot breath brushes my forehead, trips down my nose, and his chin grazes the top of my head as the world finally stills.

We stay like that, pressed against each other for a few moments more, until we hear calls from the other side of the ledge, blocked off to us by the second mini avalanche. Then Ærlen moves, peeling off me, leaving me exposed to the chill and the sight of the destruction.

The whole valley has been obliterated, trees ripped up, the cabin smashed and scattered across the valley floor.

My stomach sinks as I realise I should be dead. I would be, buried under tonnes of snow and ice, had it not been for these trolls.

Tears spring to my eyes as I think of my new reality. To everyone else, I am gone.

A sudden weight graces my shoulder, but I don't flinch. I simply turn my tear-stained face slowly to look up at Ærlen, his eyes heavy with sympathy. As I take him in, I realise yet again, that everything has changed, something in me has changed, and when he takes my hand, a deep *"Kom"* rumbling from his chest, I know that I will follow him anywhere. He leads me down from the ledge and through the trees, picking his way easily through the snow-laden branches like a lithe snow cat. I can't help but watch the way his shoulders roll with his gait, and want nothing more for those arms to be around me.

I swallow.

I should be dead, but I'm not.

My hands start to shake with the adrenaline. I need to be held, to be reminded that I am still here, alive.

I allow Ærlen to lead me though the forest and feel a jolt of electricity shoot through me as he takes my hand. There is one way to make me feel the very pinnacle of life, and that involves skin on skin, the moment of sexual release when two people become one... I don't have another person with me, but I do have a troll.

I stifle a gasp. Do I really want that? A quick glance at the green-skinned man before me sends a shudder through my core and I realise, I do. At least, I want *this* troll.

CHAPTER 13

ÆRLEN

CATHY LETS ME HELP her down from the ledge to safety but then once she is able to, she insists on walking.

I don't want to let her; she is so small and seems too shaken, but I know that if I touch her a moment longer, I may not be able to control myself.

Pressed up against her, adrenaline fuelling us, I felt something shift in me and in her — Gods, she perfumed the air with her desire, and it was all I could do just to keep her still and safe. Could it be the fabled mate bond my people speak of? Where you just know there is no life without that person?

I was almost glad when Urug called from the other side of the landslide, shushing the other women calling out to their friend. They were all safe, and they would meet us back in the longhouse as soon as we could all get there.

I dig deep inside the recesses of my brain to drag out the English I had learned at the village school.

It was a communal tongue, taught to us by teachers so old they had spoken the language themselves in the War, when our country was invaded and help from this *England* came alongside their radio broadcasts. We listened in the schoolhouse to the old transistor radio, turning the dial to the music channels whenever the teacher left the room, and pored over books, novels and newspapers that our few contacts in the outside world brought to us. But I wasn't a very good student, preferring to be outside, preparing to become leader of the Vakt.

Cathy just nods, clutching her camera bag to her, her only belongings in the world now, and follows me as I lead her through the wards and into the hidden valley, Heimli. There is a cave not far from here, set up for Vakt members on cold winter nights and after everything that has happened, tiredness is beginning to sink its claws into me.

As if reading my thoughts, Cathy stifles a yawn.

"We go to cave *nå*, and rest. There is food, fire and blankets." She doesn't reply so I continue. "Tomorrow, we go to..." I click my fingers as I search for the word. "Village."

She nods and my shoulders sink. Had I imagined our connection on the mountain? I didn't think so. Something is burning in me now that I have never felt before, consuming me with an overwhelming urge to protect and please this woman, but only if that is what she wants too.

We make it to the cave and I lead her in, my eyes better in the dark, and sit her on the ready-made bed. Then I turn and make my way to the hearth in the middle of the room, clicking the flints together on the already prepared kindling.

I stare into the flames as they grow, and then busy myself with lighting lanterns and digging out supplies, but I can't stop my thoughts.

Perhaps she is just taking time to process what happened out there. I should make her comfortable and then let her sleep. I glance over my shoulder and see her vacant expression as she stares in the flames. Yes, that must be it. I start making a stew, cutting some vegetables, gathering some snow from outside to melt as water, and throwing in some dried mushrooms and smoked meat. That should give it some flavour.

I hum to myself as I work, my tail flicking in time, and as I give the dish a final stir before placing the lid on to let it cook, I sense her behind me.

I still, not wanting to frighten her, but glance over my shoulder as she reaches out a hand and gently strokes the bushy tip of my tail. The sensation makes me jolt, and she pauses, but leaves her fingers there. Then, when she is sure I won't bite her head off, she moves her hand down and grasps the thicker sinewy part just below my tuft.

A breathy groan escapes me and she begins to slide her hand down its length.

"I've never met anyone with a tail before," she says softly, and her voice is like music to my ears after so much silence. "Is this alright?"

I turn so that I can look at her more, but not so much that I dislodge her hand, showing her the effect it has on me.

"*Ja*," I breathe, lowering my hand to my crotch and grasping my straining cock through the fabric of my trousers. "This is good."

She pauses and heat rushes to my cheeks as I think I have gone too far, but she raises her eyes from my crotch with hooded lashes and bites her lip, the corners turning up into a mischievous smile.

"How about this?" she asks as she slides one hand up to the thickest part of my tail, right at the base of my spine, and squeezes hard. I close my eyes and breathe through rounded lips, squeezing my cock to mirror her action.

"*Ja*," I growl, feeling a patch of damp spread on my trousers. Suddenly, she lets go and my eyes snap open.

She steps back and unzips her coat, the heat in the cave now raised. My own skin is burning from her touch and my hand seems to move of its own accord up and down my length as I watch her remove first her outer clothes and then, to my astonishment, reach down and drag her skin-tight polo neck upwards, exposing her navel, her ribcage and her soft, round breasts. I swallow as she pulls the rest of the top off, shaking her head a little to get the hair out of her eyes, watching how every bit of her moves in time.

Her undergarments are made of a fine blue lace and I can see the dark pink of her nipples as she turns away from me. She smiles again, and then undoes the button on her trousers, slipping them down past her wide hips, all the way down to her ankles. As she bends over, she shows me the expanse of her arse, how the lace of her panties hugs her skin, disappearing between her legs right where that fabulous scent is coming from.

"*Faen,*" I curse.

She is stunning. If I can't bury myself in her soon, I will go mad with want.

She hops out of the pile of clothes at her feet and walks over to me, her steps slow, her hips swaying alluringly. I clear my throat and motion to the furs on the bed.

"You must have clothes on. Stay warm. *Norsk vinter* is *hardt.*"

Cathy smirks and nods down at my waistline. "I can see something else that is hard."

She steps towards me again and raises her hands to un-button my white coat, biting her lip with concentration as she slips it from my shoulders and spreads her hands over my pecs through my shirt. "And, I thought you might know a good way to keep me warm."

At those words, I can't take the torment anymore and I lunge.

Chapter 14

Cathy

Without warning, Ærlen grabs my hair with his hand and presses his mouth to mine.

My head swims and I lose myself in his kiss, so powerful, so dominating and yet at the same time sensual, as if he is trying not to nip me with his fangs.

My skin burns as his other hand comes to my waist, almost encompassing it. I lean into him, breathing deeply and relishing this moment, but before I know it, he pulls back, leaving me dazed.

His eyes are heavy with desire and his chest heaves as he tries to catch his breath, testing the very limits of the seams on his linen shirt. My fingers ache to peel it off him.

"This is what you want, *på ekte*," he grumbles at himself as he searches for the English. "For real?"

He takes step back, spreading his arms wide as if to display himself, but apart from the obvious differences, such as him being green and having a tail, he is still fully clothed.

"Take your clothes off."

The words trip over my tongue before I can stop them. Ærlen nods and slowly, too slowly, reaches down for the hem of his shirt. His arms cross as he fingers the fabric and then in a ripple of hardened muscle, he pulls the shirt over his head, bunching it in his fist before throwing it on the floor by the bed.

My breathing deepens as I take in his chiselled form, every muscle I can name, and others I can't, honed to perfection in that dusky olive green, leading down from his corded neck, over the expansive chest and washboard abs to the funnel disappearing into his trousers.

Oh hell, he is perfect. I have the sudden urge to reach out and touch him, to run my fingers, no, my tongue, over such exquisite beauty, but I stop myself.

What am I doing?

My whole world has been turned upside down, and here I am trying to seduce a mythological creature from folklore. This cannot be real.

But it is. Every cell in my body yearns for him, for Ærlen, for a troll, as if there had never been an alternative. I have never felt such an acute sense of want, of need with any of the other men I had slept with, even Ed, who I had once considered spending my life with.

Ærlen seems to sense my hesitancy and stills his hand on the wooden buttons of his fly. He looks up at me, his eyes peeping from behind that bushy mop of hair, and asks again.

"This is what you want?"

I swallow, letting my feelings settle and I nod.

"Take off your clothes." I repeat my order and he obliges as I let my feelings settle. I want him so badly it feels as if my core is burning. I want this troll to sweep me up, smother me with kisses, bite anything he wants and then... Oh holy fuck!

My jaw drops as his trousers fall to the floor. He isn't wearing anything underneath and his cock springs out, bobbing in the space between us.

"Um..." I exhale, staring at the forest-green phallus aimed at me like a sword. It is enormous, probably around the size of my forearm and as thick! Ærlen bites his lip and moves his hands like he is trying to cover it up, which of course is futile.

"You don't want..." he starts, taking a half step back, but I grab his hand and pull him towards me so that the already dripping tip smears its wetness across my belly.

"Oh, trust me... I do."

True, I had never encountered a penis so large before but there was a first time for everything, right? I mean it couldn't be impossible, they sold dildos this size in most sex shops, didn't they?

He doesn't look like he believes me so I lick my lips as I look into his eyes, running my finger down his length.

"I want this..." What was it he had said? "*På ekte*, for real... I just might have to get acquainted with it first."

My stroking finger turns into a grasping hand that can't even close around his girth. A rumble vibrates around his chest as he closes his eyes, and lets me explore. I marvel at his softness, the green velvet-clad steel that responds to my touch with little jolts and judders that make me smile when his breath catches.

My curiosity is piqued as my hand travels. It isn't simply a larger green version of a human cock; there is a ridge swirling up its length interspersed with small, evenly spaced bumps or nodules. I bend down to get a closer look, grabbing his hips and turning him towards the fire so I can see better.

"What are you doing, Cathy?" he half whispers, his voice coming from a parched throat.

I kneel down, putting my head at the base of his shaft, right above his heavy bollocks, nestled in soft black curls. I grip him tightly with one hand and look up at him, a grin on my lips.

"I told you; I need to get acquainted with it."

Without leaving him any time to protest, I slip out my tongue and set it on that swirling ridge. He sucks in a curse I don't understand as I follow it up and around, sometimes flicking with the tip of my tongue, sometimes using the full width of it, catching the nodules as well. He grabs my hair to steady himself as I rip a guttural groan from him.

I look up at him. "Did I hurt you?"

I have no idea what these ridges and nodules do. He chuckles and shakes his head.

"*Nei kjaere.*" He strokes a finger down the side of my face to reassure me. "It is the opposite of hurt."

I smile and set my mouth back to his shaft, this time sucking and flicking the underside until I get to his tip. As my tongue follows the swirled ridge, I feel something wrapping itself around my thigh.

It's his tail.

It coils around my leg like a soft snake until its tuft rests in the space between them, right under the wet fabric of my panties. As I take a final long lick, our eyes meet and he raises an eyebrow, as if daring me to continue.

Well, I was never one to play chicken. I plunge his head into my mouth, the precum dripping its salty essence onto my tongue and I moan as he fills me. At that exact moment, the tufted tip of his tail flicks against the gusset of my panties and I buck. It's more solid than I thought and sends a jolt of pleasure through me, spurring me to try and take as much of him as I can in my mouth.

As I suck, his tail rubs me furiously and soon I am lost in my own passion, rocking myself between his cock hitting the back of my throat and his tail tickling my clit.

He pulls back, leaving a trail of saliva dangling between my lips and his tip. I look up at him confused, as if a trance has been broken. Is this not what he wants?

"Do you not like it?" I ask, a bit hurt, but he grins, exposing those sparkling white teeth, and nods.

"Oh, I like very much." He kneels and then lowers his mouth to my hip. With a kiss just above the thin strap of my underwear, he sinks his teeth into the fabric whilst a clawed hand rips the other side. With one deft movement he has bitten my panties from me, throwing them to the floor.

"Hey! What did you do that for?" I grumble. That was my best set, though what had possessed me to put it on tonight I would never know. Perhaps it had been thinking of him watching me in the hot tub.

Ærlen kisses my belly before flipping over onto his back and sliding his head between my legs.

"I want to taste you."

Before I can even protest, he wraps his strong arms around my thighs and pulls my pussy down on to his waiting tongue. The world tilts as he licks, flicks and sucks my clit, sighing his own pleasure as he devours me.

Oh fuck, this feels so good.

Where Ed had seen it as a chore, Ærlen seems to be really enjoying licking me out, as if my juices dripping onto his face turned him on even more.

I lean forward to reach for his cock again, but am stopped by the rigid coil of his tail whipping in front of me. It snakes round my waist and up to my tits.

I suddenly want my bra off and fumble with the clasps to allow the end of his tail to draw it off my arms. My eyelids grow heavy and my chest rises from Ærlen's tongue working me, and I marvel at his tail's dexterity. It's almost like another limb.

My head swims as it coils itself around one breast, squeezing it hard like it wants to milk me, while its tuft reaches over and flicks the other peaked nipple. I gasp and hear a small chuckle from between my legs.

Ærlen continues licking, but unwraps one of his arms from my thighs, and using a combination of his hand on the small of my back and his tail, bends me over the rod between his own legs.

My mouth is watering for it and I lap him eagerly, our paces matching. Suddenly he stops and I look down, past my tits, which are still being massaged by his tail, to see him slip two fingers into his mouth, wetting them. He winks at me as he raises his hand up over his head and eases them into my swollen labia. I open my mouth, but no sound comes out as I press back onto his fingers.

"You take my fingers well," he mutters, transfixed by the sight of me rocking back and forth onto them. I feel myself stretch around them to accommodate them. Fuck, his two fingers are already bigger than any cock I've ever ridden and it feels so good.

"More," I pant. "I need more."

Ærlen squeezes my thigh. "Soon. But *først*, you come for me, make you wet...then I slip inside you."

Jesus fucking Christ, I nearly come at those words, but then he raises his head and laps at my clit again. The stimulation is too much and within seconds, stars explode behind my eyelids and my core clenches around his fingers, squeezing them, coating them in my orgasm.

He holds me above him as I gasp for breath, letting my consciousness return to my body before slowly unwinding his tail from my waist and sliding out from beneath me and scooping me up in his arms.

His heart is pounding against my chest and I nestle into him as he carries me to one of the largest beds I've ever seen. There are a few scattered around the cave, but this one is closest to the fire and made up, ready for use.

Ærlen lays me down on the furs and presses his body against mine. He looks into my face with something...soft and powerful, and then lowers his mouth to mine. The kiss is long and slow, and delicious in its intensity. I taste myself on his tongue and combined with the huge heft pressing against my belly, it ignites my want again.

"I want you, Ærlen," I moan, opening my legs either side of him, urging him to enter.

He stills and forces me to make eye contact with him. "For real?"

Is he scared about hurting me? His size? I nod, a soft smile on my lips.

"For real, Ærlen..." I pause and tilt my head to the side. "Just take it slow."

As much as my insides ache for his cock, I don't want him to accidently bruise a kidney or something if he rams in too fast. He kisses me again and then raises himself, looking down at me splayed out before him, open and begging. He reaches down and guides his cock to my entrance.

My breath hitches and his eyes flick up to mine. I nod quickly and take a deep breath, telling myself to relax. Cautiously he presses forward, parting my lips around his tip. My eyes shut as he stretches me and my head tilts back as I gasp for breath.

The weight and pressure in my pelvis build as he inches in as far as he can. The swirling ridge that wraps itself around his cock and the small nodules tickle my insides, teasing my G spot, my A spot, O spot, all the fucking spots inside me.

I whimper and look down. He is only halfway! He must register the disappointment on my face, because he strokes my thigh, tearing his eyes away from the sight of him entering me to meet mine.

"*Flink jenta*... Good girl. You take me so well. *Åpne litt til*." His lust robs him of his English but I grasp his meaning as he presses my knees up towards my chest, opening me more, stretching me further.

Shit, I can barely breathe, but the dull sting of the stretch is muted by the overwhelming fullness that consumes me.

I want all of him, I want him balls deep in me, railing me, making me scream, so I reach out and place my hands on his hips, speeding up his entry.

"Oh yes! Fuck me, Ærlen!" My words are guttural and pleading and he needs no second bidding. He pulls out just a little and then slams into me. My scream and his roar mingle in the air as his balls slap against the curve of my arse. The sound makes him lose control and he powers into me again and again, the rhythmic slapping filling the cave.

Euphoria builds inside me as he grips my knees, pulling himself into me faster and faster. I can't take much more and grip the sheets with white-knuckled hands as he pounds another orgasm out of me. As I clench around his cock, I feel it thicken and his frantic pants turn to a roar as he comes, shooting his hot seed deep inside me.

He leans over me then, pressing his chest to mine, nuzzling his head into my neck, kissing it softly as he finishes. He pulsates, pushing more and more into me until I feel it seeping out around his cock and onto the bed sheets.

Holy fuck, how much cum was there? I get my answer as he pulls out, almost as slowly as he went in, and with each inch, another gush of hot, thick liquid spurts out of me. He doesn't seem to notice and lays on his side, wrapping me in his arms, not caring that his cum is coating both of our legs.

I try to slow my breathing and am amazed to find a chuckle escape my lips. I have just fucked, or rather have been fucked by, a troll...a frickin' troll, and it was the best sex I have ever had.

CHAPTER 15

ÆRLEN

My mind is reeling as Cathy peels herself from me, the sticky residue of our lovemaking covering her thighs.

"Is there anywhere I can clean up?" she asks, splaying her hands wide, eyebrows raised. "You trolls make quite the mess."

I laugh and prop myself up on my elbow.

"There is bathroom there." I point to a screen at the far end of the cave, still hidden in shadow. "Towels in a *kurv*." I tut and try to mimic the shape with my hands.

"Basket?" Cathy supplies.

I nod eagerly. "*Ja.*"

"And water?" She winces as I see her imagining the frigid water coming of the snowmelts. I press my lips together in a knowing smile and heave myself from the bed, my limbs like jelly after the most epic session of fucking I had ever had. Cathy looks at me suspiciously, but I won't tell her — I want it to be a surprise.

She follows me as I step into the shadows, lighting lanterns as I pass, illuminating that I, too, am covered in my seed and will need to wash after, but ladies first. We enter the small bathing area where I point out the composting toilet, essentially a bucket and urine separator that I will empty when we leave, and a brass tap jutting out of the stone wall of the cave, over a smooth stone basin.

Normally, for us, this would be a deep sink where we can sit on stools to wash our feet up to our knees, but Cathy is so much smaller that she can use it as a bath. I nod my head towards the tap encouragingly.

Cathy's mouth pulls down at the sides but reaches out and twists the knob on the top. It creaks and after a moment there is a rumble, a thunder, as the water tumbles through the pipe and suddenly, water spurts from its tip. She jumps back but I laugh and reach out my own hand, letting the warm, almost hot water run over my fingers. "Try," I encourage.

Hesitantly, and clutching one of the fluffy towels I've found for her, she stretches out her hand towards the running water. The moment she registers its temperature, her eyes light up and her lips break into the most adorably innocent smile I've ever seen on a grown woman.

"It's warm!" she cries, turning to me in her excitement. "How?"

I bend down to put the plug in and set about pulling oils and soaps from the cabinet at the side as I explain. "Hot springs in the mountain. At home, we have caves and pools for bathing." I point at the sink-cum-bath with an apologetic shrug. "But this is all here."

Cathy smiles and places a hand on my arm. My skin bursts into prickles at her touch.

"It's lovely, thanks."

That's my cue and I bow out of the space, leaving her to get clean, even though I would much rather stay and help her lather up those bewitching breasts of hers. I'll save that for the hot springs.

I throw on some trousers and a shirt despite my filth to go and check on the food. The stew has been bubbling away merrily whilst we were otherwise occupied and the cave is starting to smell divine. My stomach rumbles as if it agrees.

I hear a groan and a splash and can't help but smirk as I imagine Cathy in there, pouring water over her dark tresses, relishing its caress, but busy myself finding bowls and spoons and a half loaf that had been in my pack. It is a little squashed but still edible.

The pad of soft feet makes my ears prick up and I turn to see Cathy wrapped in a towel, which on me would only have covered my waist but instead flaps around her calves.

"I left my clothes in here," she mumbles, scurrying to the pile on the floor and pulling out the ruined scrap of fabric that had covered her arse. "Not that I can wear these again."

I wince and mutter an apology. "*Unnskyld.*"

She shrugs and turns her back to me as if suddenly shy, as if we hadn't just eaten each other like we were starved animals, but I take the hint. I clear my throat and excuse myself to wash, peeping back over my shoulder from the darkness as the towel slides down her back.

When I return, the stew is done and we sit by the fire to eat, the first helping going down in silence and then the second more leisurely. Cathy points her spoon at me.

"So...trolls exist."

I wave my own spoon before me as if to state the obvious.

"*Ja.*"

"But how? You are a myth, stories told to children—"

I stop her there and it's now my spoon being waved accusingly.

"If you speak of troll in *Bukkene Bruse*...um...three goats, he very famous bad guy. Give us bad reputation."

She purses her lips and makes a noncommittal "mmhmm" sound. I sigh and take another mouthful as I think how to answer.

"Not so many troll now, but long time ago, we lived with humans. In towns with them, mating with them, hunting, *tokt*...um...raid with them."

"Raiding? Like Vikings?"

I glower. Most modern folk consider a whole era of history as violent, its people rapists but they were farmers, woodsmen, mothers and fathers, just like the rest of us, but I let it slide.

"Yes, but men with cross and one god *kom*, push us into woods and caves. Call us monsters, creatures of devil."

I look down at my food and hit the wooden base of the bowl with my implement, but suddenly my appetite has gone.

"So, we are hunted and no choice but to hide." I look up at her and straight into her eyes. "Not just us. All trolls, huldra, nisse and fosgrim, more pushed to" — I click my fingers to get the word — "extinction and made *myte*. We are Hidden Folk."

We are silent for a moment before she places her bowl by the furs and hugs her knees. "Is that why you didn't want me to take your picture, because you are 'hidden'?"

I nod.

"If they know we live, they will hunt again. It is why we have Vakt, um, watch, to keep safe from humans."

"But things have changed." She places her hand on my arm as if to press her point home. "Norway is one of the most open countries in the world, they take care of their people. There are people from all over the world, with all colours of skin, religions, who call themselves Norwegians. Men can marry men, women can marry women—"

I cut her off.

"But must still hide sometimes."

She looks down, and her voice quivers with anger.

"Well, they shouldn't have to, and neither should you." She rocks onto her knees, placing her hands on them to get closer to me.

I turn away, looking deep into the flames. "Not important *nå*. We are the last."

"What do you mean?" She sits and places her head on my shoulder, and my tail, with a mind of its own, wraps its way around her waist. She fondles the tuft gently. I like it, and it seems to tease the words out of me.

"We are so alone, breeding with ourselves for last hundred years and *nå*, there are few I can mate with who is not...cousin or sister." I sigh, willing my brain to supply the words and the more we talk, the easier it comes from the recesses of my brain. "The same for the others. Maybe you are right, maybe world has changed. We do need more humans." I turn to her and whisper almost guiltily, "More women."

She is quiet then, and stops playing with my tuft. "Is that why..." Her words falter.

"I try to resist you, but you make it hard, standing *naken*, sucking *kuk*."

I didn't mean it to come out the way it did but as the words left my lips, I heard their arrogance and entitlement. She moves back, affronted.

"Oh, so this is my fault, is it?" A look of horror passes over her face. "What if you have put one of your troll babies in me? What the fuck do I do then? Was that your plan all along, as soon as you saw me and my friends in the woods? Kidnap us so you could pump us full of trollspawn?"

She is up on her feet now and pacing, panic consuming her, but her words hurt. I leap to my feet and grab her wrists, holding them up so she looks me in the eye.

"No! We only watch because of stone trolls crossing. It is full moon. No one should be in that *hytte*." I give her a little shake. "Would you rather be dead?"

Her breath catches and I worry I was too harsh with her, so I loosen my grip, but she doesn't move. I pull her into my arms as I whisper.

"*Ja*, I think you most beautiful woman I have seen. I would have left you, if safe, but then..." I place a finger under her chin and tilt her head up. "Up on rock, something...change."

She tenses as she takes a quick, sharp breath and I fear she will push me away again, but instead she raises her hand to my cheek.

"I know," she breathes. "I felt it too." She shakes her head, eyes closed. "I'm sorry, I should never have said those things. You saved us and..." Her eyes widen as she realises. "Oh, poor Jeppe. He's gone, isn't he?"

I nod.

"I think so. He not choose to *kom* with us, to believe. I am sorry."

She makes a noncommittal noise and rests her head on my chest. I stroke her back with my hand.

"This is just all so new and unexpected. I don't know what I am supposed to do now, Ærlen."

She looks up at me, those green eyes pleading for something. I smile gently and kiss the very tip of her nose.

"I don't know what *kommer i morgen*, but I know what you need now."

"What's that?" she says, trying to stifle a cute little yawn.

"Sleep, *kjaere*, sleep." I bend down and lace my arm under her knees and lift her, her head lolling onto my shoulder as I carry her to the bed.

Her eyes are closed before I even pull the blankets over her. The softness of the mattress and the steady rhythm of her breathing is like a spell I can't resist and before I know what I am doing, I have crawled under the sheets and lain beside her, my body pressed into her curled back and my arm resting on the swell of her hip. Just before I lose myself to sleep, I feel her grab my hand, lace her fingers with mine and pull it close to her chest.

CHAPTER 16

CATHY

THE SOUND OF BIRDS chirping wakes me and for a split second I wonder where I am, but then, the heavy pressure of Ærlen's arm over my waist reminds me.

I turn carefully towards him and take in his relaxed features. His brow is heavy and his nose is on the longer side, with a rounded snub at the end, but from it come deep, slow, contented breaths. His closed eyelids are darker that the rest of his skin, as if someone had smeared a pearlescent green eyeshadow above those long lashes that now rest on the top of his cheeks. His full lips are slack, but not open and I have to stop myself from running my finger over them, or pressing my lips to his. Although light is starting to creep into the cave, it's still dark...and cold, so I edge my way out of the bed to place another log on the fire.

As it catches and light fills the space, it falls on Ærlen and in that moment, I am aware that he is the most beautiful male I have ever seen, like a model posing for the camera, only real.

My camera. My fingers itch for it, and despite what the troll told me the night before, I have to capture his beauty. I tiptoe over to my bag and unzip it, flinching as the sound seems to echo through the cave, but my subject doesn't stir. Creeping back towards the bed, I remove the cap and place the viewfinder to my eye. I fiddle with the settings, getting the correct aperture for the lower light levels, and then, holding my breath, I press the shutter.

A horrific snapping sound fills the space and, sure enough, this one does wake the troll. He props himself up on his elbows, rubbing his eyes in such an adorable way, a way that also makes his muscles bulge, that I have to take another photo.

He realises what I'm up to and growls, his sharp fangs exposed. I snap again. He leaps from the bed, naked form towering over me, but he is magnificent in the firelight, the shadow caressing his expertly sculpted abs, thighs and... I take one last picture before he grabs my wrist, digging his claws into my flesh.

"*Stopp!*"

We stand there for a moment our panting breaths the only sound over the crackle of the flames, his with rage, mine with a bit of fear, and a little lust. I like him holding me like this, using his power and his strength, but not hurting me.

"Do you learn nothing of what I say last night? If humans see these—" He gives my hand a little shake but I interrupt him before he can continue.

"I swear I will delete them before I go...home."

Ærlen releases my wrist as my voice fades.

Home. Where was home now? Surely everyone would believe me dead after last night? I look up at my troll and see his own eyes mirroring a thought I wasn't quite ready to address, that my going home would mean leaving him here and never seeing him again.

I scoff at my own foolishness. He is a troll who saved my life, who fucked me near senseless and who I feel an inexplicable urge to climb like a tree right now, but it can't be any more than that, can it?

Surely, I can't stay here with him...can I?

I shake my head, banishing the thought, and turn to gallery mode, holding the small screen up for him to see.

"You looked so lovely, so peaceful lying there that I just had to capture you." I suck in a breath as I flick to the picture of him sleeping. "You are beautiful, and that..." I hurry on to hide my blushes. "Is what photography is all about, showing the beauty in the world."

He takes the camera from me and returns to the bed, inspecting the photo. He grunts.

"Is my nose so big?"

I laugh as the tension eases and sit beside him, helping his huge fingers to work the buttons. He looks at the last one, the one where he had rounded on me, teeth bared, and shoves the camera back at me.

"I am monster. I scare you. I am sorry."

I look down at the camera cradled in my lap and shake my head as I card my fingers through his.

"No, you are not, and you didn't. But you know what I see here? I see someone powerful, someone determined and fierce enough to protect those he loves."

It's true, he did look fierce, but in a way that makes me want him to ravage me. Ærlen purses his lips at my comment.

"But I not look...beautiful. I am troll, Cathy, I am...hideous."

I snatch my hand back, affronted on his behalf. "You most certainly are not! Do you think I would have done any of the stuff we did last night if I had thought you hideous? But..."

I stand and turn towards him, lifting the camera to my shoulder as I bite my lip. "I can take some pictures which will show you just how beautiful you really are."

He snorts but looks up from under his thatchy brown hair.

"*På ekte?*"

I grin and grab his hand, pulling him from the bed. "Really."

It doesn't take me long to get a scene set up on the floor beside the bed, using some sacks and pillows and hiding them under furs for Ærlen to lounge against. Then I turn to my model.

"Everything off," I order mischievously.

"*Hva*! You want photograph me...*naken*? *Nei*!"

I pout and walk towards him, playing with the buttons on his trousers.

"Please," I say in a slightly pitiful voice. "For me? Besides I'll cover up anything...offensive."

He runs a finger up my arm, making me shiver, and smirks, displaying one of his sharp fangs.

"What you call 'offensive'?" He chuckles and unzips my top, slipping his hand inside to fondle one of my breasts. My nipple shoots to a firm peak and I feel heat spark in my groin.

"I will be *naken*...if you are also." I raise an eyebrow but place the camera down and rip off the rest of my top. Ærlen shrugs and then drops his pants, nodding at me to do the same.

"Happy now?" I ask as I shiver a little, but if it's from the cold or anticipation, I don't know. He looks down at his crotch and shrugs.

"You tell me?"

Let's just say yes...he is definitely happy to see me standing here butt naked, save for the camera I have hung between my tits. I roll my eyes and point to the setup, throwing another log on the fire to keep the light strong.

"Sit." He does so and I bend down, moving his long legs into a position that displays their length, leading up to the fur I have placed over his manhood. "Keep that down...for now."

I smirk, grabbing his left hand and positioning it behind his head as if he is laying back on it, relaxing.

"How? When you touch me *sånn*?" I don't say anything but move his right hand onto the fur, making it hang over the swell of his thigh. It pulls the fur tighter, highlighting the rod like bulge beneath. Perfect.

I step back and look at him with my artist's eye. Where is the light falling? What is being accentuated? I take one photo of him looking at me directly in the lens, an eyebrow half raised in expectation, and then I begin to pose him, move him around, make him look into the distance.

He is a dream to work with, no embarrassment, no silli-
ness, just trusting me totally and boy, to sound cliché, but
the camera really does love him.

I stop clicking and look at my scene again.

"Take off the fur..." The words are out of my mouth
before I can stop them. Ærlen doesn't say anything, but
the corners of those dark green lips twitch as he obeys.

"Grab it."

He looks down at his ever-lengthening cock and wraps
his hand around it. I snap.

"Look at me."

He does, stroking his hand up and down the swirling
ridges, his eyes growing heavy with lust, with pleasure and
with longing.

Click.

I check the shot in the screen and my lips part. Perfection.

"Will you show me?" he asks, still handling himself, but
I shake my head and scurry over to my camera bag to find
something.

"After," I call over the camera as I slot the receiver of my
remote device into it and set up my tripod.

"After what?" His voice is a deep rumble as I step towards him, holding something in my hand.

"After you take me."

He looks at the button suspiciously.

"Take picture, or..." He grins. "Take you?"

I chuckle and straddle him, taking over the stroking of
his cock as I whisper. "Both."

Click.

Chapter 17

Cathy

Ærlen wraps his arms around my waist and in a sudden whirlwind I am on my back, my hands resting on the bulge of his muscles, looking up into his face.

Click.

I barely register the sound of the camera shutter as he lowers his head to my neck, kissing me softly, forcing my head to loll on the sack behind me, opening up for him.

I close my eyes and groan as he scrapes his fangs delicately across my skin. Click.

"I thought you were a troll, not a vampire." I try to laugh it off, but his brow furrows and I swear I hear a threatening growl of his own. As he grips the remote between his thumb and forefinger, he sits back and trails his other hand down the length of me, his tufted tail mirroring the action on the other side. They wander down my shoulders, over the swell of my breasts, pausing a while to play with my nipples, an action that makes me buzz between my legs.

I clench in response and then suddenly his hand and tail are sliding over my waist, my hips and tracing the length of my thigh, coming to a stop on my knees. Then he pushes them apart.

I am open and bare, letting this troll stare with something akin to awe at my hair-topped mound and everything underneath.

Click.

I sneak a look at the tripod and hope to God that at this angle, my leg is hiding my splayed pussy. Ærlen chuckles as he follows my gaze. He holds the remote up to the light and nods.

"This is useful."

I raise an eyebrow as he lowers himself between my legs, sticks out his tongue and takes a long, slow lap from the base of my lips to my clit. A moan is wrenched from me and as I arch my back, I hear another click.

"Yes," he pants into me, "I want to see what you look like, when I use my mouth on you. I never see that before..."

I am about to retort something about previous lovers when he dives back into me, lapping with the full breadth of his tongue before circling my clit with the very tip.

"Fuck!" Before I know it, my hands have grabbed his reed-like hair, my knuckles white as I grind my crotch into his face.

Click.

"*Sånn*," he mumbles, the vibration of his words making me tingle. He looks up at me, my arousal all over his face, and grins. "Now, I will try something. Tell me if you don't like, yes?"

I nod and ask dumbly, "What?"

Ærlen smirks again. "A little trick trolls have to get honey out of hives. So, sit *stille* and *la meg* taste your *nektar*."

I watch as he sends his long, thin tongue out between his fangs and then, to my utter disbelief, starts spinning it so fast I can't even see it anymore. He lowers it to my clit and I shriek, which makes him pull back in seconds.

"Don't stop, you idiot! Keep going!"

Assuaged, he lowers his head and does that thing again. Holy shit! Why didn't he tell me he had a vibrator in his mouth! My hips rock of their own accord now and I begin to lose myself, leaning back into the seat, dissolving.

Click.

"More, Ærlen! I need more!"

He obliges by lowering his head further so that his nose, that wonderful nose that he thinks is too big, rests on my still vibrating clit, and his tongue... Oh. My. God.

He wiggles that vibrating organ inside me. The thin tip still whirrs around madly, but the more he enters me, the thicker his tongue grows.

"Oh!" That's all I can say, my body arching, my mouth open as he fucks me with his mouth. I'm hanging on to his head for dear life as stars fill my eyes and I all but lose feeling in my legs. I barely hear the steady stream of clicks from the camera as I come, screaming, almost ripping the hair from his head.

He carries on as I ride my orgasm, slowing bit by bit alongside me, first stopping the vibration but still thrusting, his nose rubbing my clit as his tongue fills my core. Then, he retracts, but keeps his head nestled against my pelvis until I am steady enough to let go of his hair and slump back, sucking in air to calm my rapidly beating heart. He sits back and wipes his slick mouth with the back of his hand before pointing at the camera.

"*Kan jeg se?*"

I nod and he rises, hard erection leading him over to the display panel. He taps and scrolls through the pictures he has taken.

"*Faen!*" he exclaims, grabbing his cock. "*Du er så jævla nydelig.*"

I have no idea what he is saying but when he turns to look back at me, his eyes are dark with lust. "*Jeg vil knulle deg.*"

I shrug and sit up, feeling finally returning to my limbs. "What?"

He is suddenly between my legs, his heft pressing into my slick heat, its tip leaking a silvery trail over my belly as he nips my earlobe and growls.

"I want..." He grabs my hands and using his tail as a restraint, holds them above my head, allowing his hands to wander over my breasts. "...to fuck you."

My breath catches. I want nothing more, but then my eyes fall on the camera and I shake my head.

"Ah, ah, ah..."

Confusion washes over his features as I wrench my hands free and push his hard chest back.

"It's my turn." I wriggle out from underneath him and place him back where he had been for our photoshoot and grab the remote from his hand. Then with a quick check of camera angles, I am back, climbing onto his lap, his spiralled cock rubbing between my legs.

"It's my turn to watch you come," I say as I place my hands on his broad shoulders to steady myself. His tail curls itself around my waist to help support me as I rise on my knees and reach down to grasp his cock.

He judders as I squeeze it, forcing a small laugh from his lips.

Click.

"Why not both?" he whispers, throwing his head back as I place the tip of him inside my wet cunt.

Click.

My mouth opens like his in a silent scream of pleasure as I ease myself down, over his ridges, widening, stretching to accommodate him. I look down and see that I'm only half-way, but I need a break, a moment to acclimatise to this heft I am lowering myself onto.

He senses my hesitation and shifts under me so he can set his thumb on my clit, rotating it gently. It eases me instantly and I hover there, relishing the delicious swirls, letting my muscles relax.

I take a deep breath and press down, closing my eyes as I am opened fully, impaling myself on him until I reach the base.

Click.

Our groans of pleasure harmonise and echo around the cave. When I open my eyes, they lock onto Ærlen's and I rock my hips, watching his eyelids flutter.

He fills me so entirely; I almost feel stuck on him but with each rock it becomes easier. He reaches out and grabs my hips, helping me to move on him, lifting me slightly so that he can scoop his hips up in time with my movement, making sure I feel ALL of him.

Click.

My hands slip down from his shoulders to his chest, receiving a quick kiss on my inner arm as they travel and I pin him in place, my rocking taking on a mind of its own now, a rhythm I am not in control of. A rhythm that works me hard, sending a trickle of sweat down my back as my head begins to swim.

I have never felt so alive, so in control and yet so utterly helpless to my own urges.

Click.

I'm close now, and from the shortened pants underneath me, it won't be long for him either. I reach back behind me, placing my hands on his knees, throwing my head back as I thrust my hips up further, harder, fucking him as I ride up and down his spiralled ridge.

He bellows and begins to thrust up into me with such speed, all I can do is hold on for dear life...and press the remote with a series of frantic clicks as we both finish and I spasm and writhe on top of him.

He explodes into me with a series of long, sharp upward thrusts, his eyes shut, his face scrunched up in that awkward mix of pleasure, of release, but pain that it is now over.

My core clenches around him, pushing his spunk back down gravity's path. I feel it spilling out of me and all over him; his thighs, his stomach, probably dripping down past his balls too, and that's not even the half of it. The rest is still in me, plugged up by his hardly diminishing cock.

Slowly, I set my feet on the floor and raise my arse, pulling myself off him, each inch making me feel hollow and empty. He falls out with a gush of his cum, which spatters all down my thighs and onto the furs, almost as if I had birthed something and I have the sudden, horrifying thought of actually birthing a troll baby. I cough and look down at the mess.

"Time for another bath, I think."

Ærlen sighs and nods. "*Ja*, I will clean the cave, make it...fit for others, and then we leave."

"Leave?" I spin on my heel and look at him dumbly.

"To go back to village, meet with your friends?" There is a questioning tone to his voice, as if asking whether I had forgotten them. And truth be told, I had. I had been so swept up by Ærlen and his scent and his all-singing, all-dancing cock, that I had completely forgotten that my friends were out there somewhere, and that this cave was not my final destination. I look around the sanctuary a little forlornly. I will miss this place. Once we step outside of its walls, a decision will have to be made. Would I rush back to humanity, civilisation, and tell everyone I wasn't dead, going back to a life of uncertainty? Or would I choose to stay in a forgotten corner of Norway, with a troll who makes me see stars?

CHAPTER 18

ÆRLEN

WE HAVE WALKED QUITE far along the mountainside and into the valley before we stop for a rest. I lead her to a break in the trees and we sit, chewing on some *speke* — strips of dried meat.

The whole valley is laid out before us. Just below, smoke rises from the long-house roofs of my village, and the calls and shouts of the villagers going about their lives drift up to us. Further down the length of the shores of the lake that serves us with fish, the dark shapes of another village sit against the snowy white back-drop. The sky is brilliantly clear again and Cathy closes her eyes as she lets the sun kiss her skin.

"Let me see," I say, nudging her elbow and shattering her peace. Without needing to ask what, she reaches into her pack and pulls out the camera. We spend a while, heads bent together inspecting the evidence of our lovemaking. I grow hard watching, entranced by the way my green skin and her pale limbs fit together so easily, but I barely look at myself.

My eyes are simply for her, roaming over her curves, her openness, the way she closes her eyes and tilts her head back in a silent moan. I grunt and fiddle with my trousers which are suddenly too tight. I want to go again, I want to rip her clothes from her now and make her make that face again, but the village and her friends wait down below, so I shift away from her, trying to hide my arousal.

"You are right. Pictures can be beautiful." I am talking about her. She is beautiful. Yes, I am pleased with how athletic and strong I look, but it is her that makes those photos art.

"They are," she sighs, tucking her instrument back in its coverings. "It's one of the reasons I wanted to come on this trip. Get some more practice, capture some landscapes, wildlife..." She smirks as she nudges my shoulder. "And, I had hoped to capture the Northen Lights, but...well your stone trolls put a stop to that. I've always wanted to see them, and I just thought if I had a couple of really good shots for my website, then people will think I am a real photographer, legit."

I reach for her hand.

"You are very good. The pictures of us...they are..." I try to copy her words, but my accent makes them sound thick and dumb. "Legit."

She snorts and picks up another piece of *speke*. "Yeah sure, if I want to shoot pornos."

I don't really know what she is talking about, but I don't want to show my ignorance. As much as we know about the outside world, there are some things, words, that have passed us by, especially in other languages.

"Don't worry," she mutters. "I'll delete them too."

She doesn't say "when I leave" but it hangs in the air between us. She points towards the village with the half-chewed strip of jerky in her fingers.

"Tell me about your village. Is there something I must do, like bow to a leader and beg his mercy or something, otherwise you throw me in a pot and boil me for your suppers, grind my bones to make your bread?"

I scoff. "Now, you confuse us with giants."

She grins and the dread that had filled me with the idea of her leaving eases. "We have leader, yes, a Jarl, but he is old. He waits to choose who will follow."

Cathy licks her fingers as she finishes her mouthful and I can't help but watch them slide out of her wet lips with jealousy.

"So why doesn't he?" She raises an eyebrow. "There seem to be enough of you young male trolls, cavorting round the woods."

I roll my eyes at her and balancing my elbows on my knees, I clasp my hands together.

"The next Jarl must be from *Dalvakt*, we who protect the valley, and..." I incline my head a little sheepishly. "It is *oft* leader — Sjef." The penny drops.

"Ah, and that would be you? Congratulations!" She claps my back, beaming at me. I shake my head.

"It is not so easy. Jarl must be strong, fearsome warrior but must *balansere* with a second voice, calmer, wiser. None wiser than women behind strong men."

"And there are no women to be your mates." She repeats what I had told her last night, that we were on the brink of extinction. I don't look at her, I can't, suddenly afraid that I will see hurt and betrayal in her eyes. Would she assume again that my team and I had taken the human women from the mountain for that sole purpose? True, my actions with her hadn't exactly done much to counter that thought. The Gods only knew, she could be carrying my child as we sit here in silence.

Finally, she turns her knees towards me and begins to talk, more to herself, as if she is sorting out the pieces of a puzzle.

"And you can't go out to find women, because you are scared they will make you some sort of freak show, or hurt you?"

I nod. "There are some humans, know and help us, bring goods and news, but are old now, from long ago, when again Hidden Folk and humans work together to save this land. When they die..." I swallow. "We die also."

Another pause and Cathy runs her fingers through her dark tresses. "And we just happened to come to your valley, right at this critical moment, four single girls...well, three who would mate with a troll, anyway."

I raise an eyebrow, wondering which of them preferred her own sex, but get no answer. Cathy blows out her cheeks, exhaling loudly and taking deep breaths like she is trying to calm herself. I reach out and rest my hand on her juddering knee.

"Am I your mate now? After what we have just done — does that mean..."

I grab her hands and stroke the side of her face, trying to keep her calm. "We created mate bond, *ja*, but...you only my mate, if it is something you want. There is ritual to complete the bonding of mates, like your..." I click my fingers and tsk as I think of the word, but she supplies it for me.

"Marriage?"

I nod. "*Ja.*"

She slips her hand from mine and shrinks in a little on herself. Hurt sparks in my chest as she looks up at me warily.

"And is that what you now want, with me? I'm not sure if I am ready for that." She stands and begins to pace, waving her hands around as her voice rises in pitch. "I've just gone through a horrible break-up with the guy I always thought I would be marrying and having kids with but, like many, many years from now."

I watch her feet as she gets closer and closer to the edge, rising to my own feet cautiously, arms outstretched so I don't frighten her.

"But shit!" She turns as the thought that had gone through my mind hits her. "I could actually be..." She doesn't finish as her foot spins and her heel slips off the edge of the mountain.

I'm there before she has time to scream, cradling her in my arms and pulling her back from the edge. Her hands rest on my chest and she looks up at me, terror written across her face, but whether from the near fall or the possible pregnancy, I don't know.

"*Alt* is your choice, Cathy. I will not make you to do anything." She nods and I am about to let her go, when she grabs the collar of my coat.

"And if I decide to leave? What happens then?"

I suck in a breath.

"Memory and *kamera* will be" — I wipe one palm over the other, not knowing the word — "clean and you can go."

She shakes her head.

"So, I won't remember anything? Not even...you?"

Are those tears brimming in the corners of her eyes? I swallow, something hard suddenly stuck in my throat, and nod.

"Sage mother, who makes you forget, make it seem like you just wake up in forest after avalanche. We leave you near human village to find help. *Men...nei.*" I shake my head. "You will not remember trolls, our problem...or me."

But I would, and it would haunt me until the end of my days. She loosens her grip on my collar and steps back. I let my arms drop and watch her pick up her camera bag, slinging it over her shoulder, and wrap her arms around her as if she was hugging herself.

"I..." She stops herself with a shaky inhale and then raises her red-rimmed eyes to mine. "I need to think...and I guess there are some things I need to discuss with my friends. Can you take me to them...please?"

I bow my head, pick up our meagre belongings and trudge back into the forest, aware of the crunch of her boots on the snow as she follows.

CHAPTER 19

CATHY

WE WALK SLOWLY AS I mull things over in my head. Ærlen doesn't talk now, respecting my need for silence, but I can see from the way his tail trails along the snow behind him that he is upset.

What does he expect me to say? That I love him? That I want to spend the rest of my life with him? That's absurd...isn't it? But as my thoughts drift back to that moment on the ledge, the pull I felt towards him, the way everything had just felt so right...I know this bond between us is real. My thoughts are shattered as a noise breaks through the woodland quiet.

It is loud and thundering high above — the whirr of rotor blades. I crane my neck and try to see through the canopy but the sound of the helicopter must be coming from the neighbouring valley.

"They're looking for us!" I cry, my head snapping to Ærlen's. "We have to go back!"

His eyes dim at my words and his shoulders sink a little, but he shakes his head. "*Nei*, we go to village, meet with friends. They will worry for you."

He sucks in a breath and turns back down the path.

"You can decide together if you go back to human world."

I have to scurry to keep up with him, my breath fogging in the cold air. He's right. I can't just turn back now. We have no more food, no supplies, and I want to make sure my friends are alright. We need each other now, more than we ever have done.

As the mountainside slopes downwards, the trees thin and before I know it, the sounds of village life fill my ears. I pause on the edge of the treeline and peer at the community of trolls and their strange women folk, beautiful with cow-like tails, going about their business. How would they react to me? Would I be welcomed or shunned as a human?

"Cathy?" Ærlen puts a hand on my shoulder and it's only then that I realise my knuckles gripping the branch in front of me are white. "All is well." He holds out his hand. "You are safe with me."

Fear wells up inside me and I extend a shaky hand to take his. As soon as his fingers close around mine, I feel relieved. He is right. He has protected me this far. I have to trust him. Slowly we walk out of the treeline and all eyes are drawn to us. As the trolls and huldra stare at me, I stare back and my fingers tighten around Ærlen's.

I almost can't believe what I am seeing. The village is made up of long and round huts, fashioned the very same way they must have been over a thousand years ago. I could have been mistaken for thinking I had walked into one of those historical attractions, the Viking villages, had it not been for the almost seamless blend of items from across the centuries, the first of which were the wrought-iron lamp posts, flames flickering behind sooty glass.

I stare in bewilderment at the town's folk, some wearing almost historical clothes, long skirts and shawls, others sporting the patterned, knitted sweaters like Jeppe had worn, and bobble hats barely hiding their bushy hair.

A bug-eyed tractor that looks like it's right out of the 1940s sits alongside a flock of sheep, and hens stroll in and out of the buildings.

Then a shout goes up and we are welcomed with smiles and calls for help, and I soon find myself bundled into a thick woollen blanket by a grey-haired huldra woman, still startlingly beautiful despite her advanced years. They chatter away in their native tongue and my head is beginning to swim with each step we take towards the enormous black wooden-walled building in the centre of the village, when a familiar figure, long blonde hair flowing behind her, comes running out of it. I throw off the blanket with joy as she calls my name.

"Cathy! Oh, thank God you're alright!" Sam crushes me in her iron embrace, wetting my face with tears of relief and it's only as she steps back that I realise I am crying too.

"I'm fine. I'm fine," I say somewhat dumbly, as if they are the only words I know. I glance over my shoulder at Ærlen who is standing a little way back, arms crossed, giving us space for our reunion. "I have been well looked after."

My cheeks flush. God, if she only knew. My teeth are chattering and as Sam picks up the blanket and rearranges it around my shoulders, I notice that the others aren't there.

"Sam? Where are Lauren and Izzy?"

The tall, slender woman at my side sighs and motions with her head to the doorway.

"Come on, let's get you warmed up and fed."

I let her lead me into the dim light of what appears to be a Viking longhouse, a huge firepit running down the centre, with long, heavy wooden tables and benches on either side. The strange mix of ancient and more modern items continues. I spy a beautifully painted grandfather clock in the corner, oil lamps on the walls, enamel tins on the counter-tops, and even a bookshelf. But everything has a patina of age about it, as if nothing is newer than the middle of the twentieth century.

Children run about playing and huldra women in long skirts scold them as they get too close to the fire. At my arrival there's another flurry of movement and before I know it, I have been wrapped up, placed in a chair by the fire and a large bowl of soup set in my hands.

My hunger gets the better of me and I dive into it, burning my mouth as I inhale the simple but delicious meal.

As soon as I am sated, I wipe my mouth on the back of my hand, place the wooden bowl down and grab Sam's hand.

"Now, where are Lauren and Izzy? I thought you were all together, has something happened to them?" The sour taste of dread coats my mouth now, but vanishes when Sam shakes her head.

"They are fine...at least I think they are. Lauren was having some contractions, so that big bald one took her to some sort of midwife, I think. They should be back soon, but I guess she may have been told to rest for a while."

I let out a deep breath, some of the tension easing from my bones. I glance back at the doorway where Ærlen has just walked in, head bent as he talks with the troll and huldra who had brought Sam back. His eyes meet mine and I am filled with a rush of want for him. The firelight and the shadows of the long hut make him appear something from a legend.

"And Izzy?" I force myself to turn back to Sam who has followed my gaze with a raised eyebrow.

"Well, you know Izzy and the guide, Jeppe, were basically fucking?"

How could I not? They had been all over each other. I nod.

"Well, she was frantic, said we had to go back and look for him, that he needed our help."

I sit back, my mouth open. "But there is no way he could have survived that, is there?"

Sam shakes her head, her golden ponytail swishing round her cheeks. "No. Fritha and Vedlun say not, and Torak, the one who carried Izzy away from the cabin, he tried to tell her, but she wouldn't have any of it. So, they went back to look for him."

"Oh." I fall silent. If they went back, perhaps the helicopters had seen her, perhaps she had been rescued...but wait. Ærlen had said if they wanted to leave, their memories would be wiped, but that has to be done by a sage mother. Torak is part of the Vakt too, there is no way he would let Izzy run back to humanity and tell them all about the trolls. Sam grabs my hand, following my thoughts.

"They will be back soon," she says, but her voice wavers.

I sit back and stare into the fire, a sudden exhaustion washing over me. My eyelids are closing when a familiar hulk bends over me, slipping his strong hands under my legs and back. It's Ærlen. His scent fills me as I lay my head against his chest.

"I'm tired, Ærlen," I say as he carries me away from the fire. "I don't want to go outside again right now." He chuckles softly and it's like listening to a lion purr.

"You sleep here. With women." In a few short strides, he has carried me to the low eaves of the longhouse where cots are nestled the length of the building. Using his tail, he whips back the embroidered blanket and lays me down on the crisp linen sheets. I shiver at their coolness but he tucks me in and places a warm hand on my head. I nuzzle into him and as he turns to leave, I cradle his hand like a teddy bear.

"Stay with me," I murmur, not wanting to be left alone with these women, these strangers, no matter how reassuring their smiles. Ærlen crouches low so that his face is level with mine. He leans in and touches the tip of my nose with his, brushing it back and forth with a smile.

"I also must sleep, Cathy, and I am unmated male..." He coughs. "I must go to the *Ungkar hytte*." His eyes twinkle, even if his smile is sad. "But I rather stay with you, have you warm my *kuk* with *rumpe* in sleep."

I look around nervously, but giggle when I realise no one has heard. Ærlen laughs too.

"*Sov*, sweet Cathy." I love the way his long thin tongue pokes from his teeth as he says my name, "I will be here when you wake."

As he hauls himself up on the wooden sides of the cot, he kisses me delicately on my forehead, and as if his lips possess some kind of magic, I drift off to sleep in seconds.

CHAPTER 20

ÆRLEN

It's cold in the *Ungkar hytte* — the cabin for those of us unmated males — and as I toss and turn on my bed, as tired as I am, sleep won't come. There is something...someone missing, and it's as if my body is agitated by her absence.

After a few hours where I drift in and out of an uneasy sleep, I make my way back to the longhouse, unable to stay away a moment longer.

As soon as my eyes adjust, I scan the gloom, and make out the shape of three women at the end of the room, all chattering merrily, laughing from time to time. Cathy's smile makes the corners of my own mouth prick up, but the smile is wiped from my face when a solid hand claps my shoulder and a deep voice rumbles in my ear.

"Good to see you safe, Ærlen," Urug leers down at me, speaking in our own tongue. "I almost thought that you wouldn't make it back." I shrug him off and nod.

"I made it back before you."

The large troll beside me runs a hand over his bald head and smirks.

"Yes, well Lauren and I stopped at the sage mother's, just to make sure the child was well and...she had other things that needed seeing to."

I don't want to look at him, but my curiosity gets the better of me and my eyes slide to his. Urug chuckles.

"You know what they say when the females reach a certain time in their pregnancy...they are crazy for it...and I can tell you—"

I raise a hand to stop him. I don't want to hear the sordid details. Suddenly, the twinkle in his eye vanishes and he steps in front of me, squaring off and staring down his bulbous nose at me.

"I thought you would be happy for me, *bror*, to find a mate again after..."

My jaw drops. "She has agreed to be your mate?"

Urug's top lip turns up in a half snarl. "Not yet, but she will. She has nothing to go back to and she wants a father for her child." He jabs a finger in my chest. "And when she says yes, what is to stop Haldor naming *me* the next Jarl? After all, I will already have a woman, and a family."

Rage boils up in me. He is always trying to prove he is better than me, stronger, just because he is older. "Do you even care for her, or is this just some sick scheme to best me and become Jarl?"

Before I know what is happening, his forearm is pressed against my throat and my back is slammed against the wall. Gasps and then silence rings from those in the hall at the sudden violence and before he can even speak, a strong but ageing voice booms around the space.

"Desist!"

Reluctantly, Urug lowers his arm and as he backs away, my eyes fall on Cathy and her friends, who have made it to the front of the crowd. Her brows are furrowed and her thoughts unreadable.

"You embarrass yourselves in front of our guests like a pair of *ungdom*." Jarl Haldor taps his cane on the slate tiles of the floor. I rub my throat but apologise, as does Urug, before the pregnant human, Lauren, rushes to his side and hisses something I can't hear up at him.

Haldor must see my eyes narrow at the sight of them, nods once and then sighs. "Let us eat, and we will discuss whatever grievances you have on the morrow."

As much as he has been grooming me to follow in his footsteps, if Urug has a mate and I do not, if Cathy decides to leave, then tradition dictates that he will have to pass me over in favour of a family man.

I nod and stalk towards the long tables set up around the fire-pit in the centre. Thankfully, Urug's woman leads him to the other side. The bench bounces a little as Cathy sits beside me.

"Do you want to tell me what that was about?"

I don't need to. My eyes slide to the troll-human couple, now nuzzling against each other and whispering sweet nothings as though they were youths who had just discovered what their genitals did.

"Ah," she says. "So, you know about Urug and Lauren. Yes, she told us they got friendly on the way here..." I growl but she places a hand on my knee under the table. "Just like we did."

Her words pull my eyes to hers and as they twinkle in the firelight, my bad mood dissolves, though not entirely disappearing. She is right. We did get friendly, and not knowing if she will stay or go, I want to enjoy every single moment I can with her.

"You are right. I am sorry for my aggression."

Cathy shrugs. "I dunno, it was kind of hot seeing you all growly."

I scoff and lean into her while she picks up her beer mug. "Oh, you want me to be like that...with you?"

She pretends to think about it in an overexaggerated way and then shakes her head. "I don't know...we'll have to try it and see."

I stifle a groan as I take my own swig of ale and we tuck into our meal, forgetting the disturbance of a few moments ago.

Suddenly, the door bursts open and as the cold air of the Norwegian night blows in, two figures enter. Before I can see who it is, Cathy is on her feet alongside the tall blonde one and is rushing to the final member of their group who has arrived with Torak, whose wild hair and beard are covered in snow. There is no one else with the troll and the human woman.

"Come in! Shut that door!" a matronly huldra shouts from the head of the table. It is Tuva, Haldor's mate. She stands and looks down from her raised seat at the four women embracing.

"What news, Torak?" She speaks in clear English, as many of my kind do, and not for the first time do I curse my inattentiveness in class.

The troll is taller than me but more gangly with longer, almost weed-like hair that falls past his green ears. He shakes his head, but steps forward and places a small item on the table.

"We found the guide." His voice is a growl.

I glance at Izzy's face. Her lip is wobbling.

"He was dead."

My heart sinks, yet I knew deep down that it had to have been true. Cathy clutches at Lauren's shoulders.

"We found his phone." Torak points to the small black box on the counter. Everyone seems to lean in, looking at the shiny rectangle.

"Why have you brought this here? You will lead them to us!" Haldor jumps up from his seat, waving his stick in the air. His mate holds out a hand to calm him.

I glance at Cathy and see that her eyes are wide with what looks like fragile hope. The girl, Izzy, steps forward.

"I brought it. I thought..." She glances up at Torak and bites her lip before continuing. "I wanted to keep up to date with the news, since my phone was destroyed. There are helicopters circling the area."

We had heard as much, but the fact that they had actually seen the great metal birds and could have been seen by the humans riding in them sends a chill down my spine. Lauren rises from her place on the bench, placing a hand on her belly as if to protect the unborn child. Perhaps she was just comforting herself.

"And what is the news?"

All eyes turn to Izzy. She glares up at Torak with heat in her eyes, her lips thin.

"I don't know. As soon as he knew I had it, he took it off me. The last I saw was that they had launched a rescue mission."

Tuva walks around the table slowly and picks up the phone. She taps it against her hand and then holds it out to the human.

"Check it again." The silence in the longhouse deepens and Cathy whimpers as she watches her friend take the shiny device and switch it on. Her face is suddenly lit up by the blue light from the screen and the colours shift as she taps and types and then starts swiping her finger furiously. She stops and clicks again. Her eyes scan the screen but then her brow furrows.

"I can't understand it...there doesn't seem to be enough signal here and the translation wont load." She holds the phone up for Tuva. The old huldra takes it, holding it out before her to see better despite her failing eyesight and begins to read.

"'Latest update on the Dysterdal avalanche. One body has been found. Male, in his thirties. The search continues throughout the night as the window to find survivors closes, but as temperatures plummet and the light fades it will be difficult for the rescue team to continue due to the damage the avalanche caused. As well as the destruction of the luxury *hytte*, trees and rocks have also been dislodged and the snow itself is very unstable. It has now been over 24 hours since the accident, and experts say that if no survivors are found by morning, it is unlikely any of the women will have survived and the search will be called off.'"

Her voice falls and she places the phone back on the table. We stare at it until the light fades and the screen turns to black once more. No one dares speak, but I hear sobs coming from the other side of the table and see Lauren run to Urug and hide her face in his chest. Cathy withdraws into herself.

"They think we are dead." The tall blonde one, Sam, stands and walks over to where the phone has been placed on the table. She reaches for it, her voice becoming high-pitched with panic. "We need to call someone, let them know we are alive!"

"No!" Haldor shouts, and raises his cane above his head. He brings it down with a crack on the phone, smashing the screen and crushing the device entirely.

"What did you do that for?!" Sam screams, sinking to her knees, picking up the shards of the phone, tears welling in her eyes. "We could have been saved!"

Fritha rushes to her side and holds her as she dissolves into tears.

"They think we are dead."

"You should never have brought that device here in the first place. We may not use them, but we know all about your modern technology with its tracking devices. The last signal that phone will have sent out will be from here. You could have exposed us all!" Haldor spins round to his mate, his fangs bared. "Why did you let them use it?"

She sighed. "Because it was already here, the signal has already been recorded; you may as well let them know their fate."

Cathy looks up at me, eyes pleading, but I don't know what she wants. She walks over to her friend on the ground. The others join their huddle and they look up at Tuva.

"So that's it, we are stuck here forever?" Izzy asks imploringly, her full bottom lip wobbling. The Jarl's mate shakes her head and my stomach clenches as she explains the choice they have to make.

"No. While we welcome you here with open arms, there is still a way you can return to civilisation, but it involves sacrifice. You must give up any memory you have of your time here, of us. The sage mother has potions that will wipe your memory back to the first moment you saw a troll. If you decide to take it, you will fall into a deep sleep and will be carried back to the edge of the disaster site by sled. They will find you at dawn, before the search is called off.”

She looks at the door and the darkness beyond it. I glance at the ancient grandfather clock in the corner. It goes dark early here in the Norwegian winter, but I know that in order to get them back before dawn, they will only have a few hours to decide.

“You must decide by midnight.”

She holds out a hand to help Cathy up. She in turn helps her pregnant friend to stand, while short, curvy Izzy and Fritha haul a distraught Sam to her feet, her long limbs turning gangly with her grief. The wise huldra’s head turns and she seems to be staring right at me and Urug.

“If I were you, I would use these last hours wisely. It seems bonds have been forged that are so easily broken.”

Chapter 21

Cathy

Ærlen holds out his hand towards me but I shake my head.

"You brought me here to talk with my friends." I take a long breath in. "And that is what I must do."

My troll leans in close and as his scent washes over me, I want nothing more than to melt into him. "But our bond? We must talk of this."

I hear the panic in his voice and place a hand on his arm. "And we will, but right now, I need to know what they intend to do."

I don't give him chance to dissuade me and make my way over to where Sam has been bundled into a rocking chair by the fire.

Izzy is perched beside her, patting her hand and for once, her words aren't laced with jealousy, only kindness.

"Come on, it's alright. We'll figure this all out."

Sam shakes her head and turns her tear-stained face up to Fritha.

"Would you mind giving us some space?"

The ethereal beauty of the huldra dims for a second in her disappointment at being dismissed, but she nods.

"Of course. I'll be right over there, if you need me."

We are quiet, simply sitting and holding each other's hands until Lauren, who has been talking with a huldra, who I assume from all the pointing at her belly is the healer, walks towards us, head down. She sits slowly, leaning on the back of the chair and almost disappearing into the shadows that cling to the corner.

"What are we going to do?" I ask tentatively.

Sam's head snaps up, her mouth open and her brow furrowed in disbelief.

"We go home! What else would we do?" She runs a finger through her hair, dislodging the beautiful braid that makes her look like one of the huldra herself. "We take that motherfucking potion and we forget all of this and go back to our lives."

I flinch at the thought of returning to what had been my life. The shame, the betrayal, the terrifying thought of starting all over again.

"Perhaps *you* can." Lauren's voice cracks as tears fall down her face. In an instant, Sam's harsh expression melts and she slips to the floor before the mother-to-be.

"Lauren? What are you saying?" Sam's voice is full of worry.

"If I take that potion, it won't just be my memories I lose." She sniffs and places her hands protectively on her belly. "It will be my baby, too."

"Oh Lauren!" Izzy's hand shoots up to her mouth, her bright blue eyes dimmed with tears. My own throat clogs with the horrific choice presented to her. It is no choice at all really.

Lauren shakes her head and wipes her nose on her sleeve. "So, I will be staying...with Urug. He has been kind to me. Says he will protect us both, and I... I believe him."

"But Lauren..." Sam grips her hand, a silent plea, a personal one in her eyes. Lauren ignores it.

She heaves herself to her feet, letting Sam slip to the floorboards. "You must do what is right for you, but if you choose to stay, then I will be happy to have my friends here with me."

She can't look us in the eye as she leaves, scurrying into the enormous bald troll's embrace as he ushers her outside.

"Well?" I ask, my heart pounding in my chest. "What about you two?"

Sam's jaw tightens and she shakes her head, her eyes filled with tears. "No. I have a life to get back to. I am an athlete. I have the world championships coming up... I cannot... I will not stay here."

"Not even for Lauren?" Izzy almost shouts. "We can't just leave her here! Or are you just that self-obsessed, that all you care about is winning some stupid title?"

Sam is on her feet now, her fists clenched. I jump up and put myself between them.

"Stop this!" I hiss. "Lauren didn't have a choice, but we do, and we must do what we think is right, for ourselves. Sam, if that is leaving for you..." I wrap my arms around her and she softens a little. "Then I wish you all the best."

I step back and the two blonde women, one tall and slender, the other short and curvaceous, stare at me.

"So, you are staying too?" Izzy asks, something akin to incredulity mixed with hope in her voice as her eyes slide to the lithe, long-haired troll leaning against a bookcase. He has a book open in his hands, but he isn't reading it, he is looking at her.

I shrug and look over my shoulder at Ærlen who is pacing the floor, waiting for me. "I don't know. There is someone I need to talk to first."

Chapter 22

Cathy

I follow Ærlen dumbly out of the long hut and into the dark winter evening. My breath fogs as I let out a long shaky breath, trying in vain to hold back the tears.

I had known, deep down, I had known this would be the outcome, that I would have to make a choice, but now that I have to make it, I don't want to.

It should be an easy one to make — take the potion, forget the trolls and go back to humanity, back to our lives as they were, yet somehow it isn't so simple.

Ærlen takes my hand and leads me back out of the village.

"Where are we going?" I sniff up at him as he places my camera bag on my shoulder. He stops and sets his finger under my chin, tilting my head so that I can't help but look up into his large black eyes. He smiles, but it looks sad.

"We go to take *fotos*, ones you can keep...if..." He can't bring himself to say it. Of course, my camera will also have to be wiped of any evidence that the trolls exist. I nod, and he leads me through the trees, dappled moonlight shining through the canopy whilst I sift through my thoughts. What was I going to do?

I couldn't imagine what my parents would be going through, waiting for news of me, only to be told in a few hours that I was dead. Maybe they already thought I was. They were like that...practical, assessing the facts. They had never been unkind parents, and they loved me very much, but they had let me find my own way in the world, and apart from meeting up at Christmas and other family events, it was only a weekly phone call with my mother. Whilst I don't want them hurting, would it make much difference to our lives if I don't return?

The ground gets steeper now and I clutch at Ærlen as he half drags me up the mountainside, leaving the safety of the trees for a slope of pure rock. It is slippery in places where the ice clings to it, but the big troll has sure feet and soon we are level again. My eyes drift down to the moonlit valley and I take a deep breath. It is so quiet here, so peaceful. No constant rush to try and do something, earn money, be 'someone'. That's all that waits for me back home, isn't it? Especially as I would be starting all over again, making a name for myself in a different field, a different town. Because I couldn't stay where I had been, not when Ed was there with his new wife. Ed.

My heart clenches as I think of him. Did he know I had gone missing? Would he even care?

I bunch my mittened hand into a fist and set my mouth in a straight line. Why should I care what he is going through? He used me, broke my heart and threw me aside like a piece of rubbish. If he had any feelings left for me, then let him feel them now. Now that I'm gone. I stopped short at that thought. Was I gone?

"Here." Ærlen's voice breaks me out of a trance and my head snaps up. In the light of the moon, I make out that we are on a large clifftop, the valley splayed out beneath us. There are tree stumps arranged around an unlit firepit and a slumped shelter sits further back, its front open to the view. I shiver.

Ærlen, standing on the edge of the platform and silhouetted against the starry backdrop, places his hands on his hips and shakes his head. He looks magnificent, like something from a fairytale, prince and monster rolled into one. Then he bends to light a fire.

"No." I hold out a hand to stop him. "Fire will affect the light." I walk over to him slowly, a little afraid of how the rock face vanishes at such a sharp angle, and loop my arm through his.

"What exactly have we come to take pictures of? Even with this moon, it's pretty hard to see anything through the lens."

The troll at my side shoots me a sideways glance, the corner of his mouth crooked with a smile. He kneels and pulls me onto his other knee so I am sitting, and points up at the sky.

"Even this?"

I scoff, thinking he is talking about the smear of stars, which yes, would make a lovely photo with no light pollution anywhere, when my breath stops. There is a tiny flicker in the distance and I shake my head.

"Is that...?"

Ærlen doesn't need to say anything because suddenly the sky erupts into colour. Blues, greens, pinks and purples, all swirling together, chasing each other between the stars.

"The Northern Lights!"

My eyes fill with tears and I lean my head back against his shoulder, and for several moments we sit there, our cheeks touching, looking up at the astounding beauty of nature.

"Cathy?" he whispers. "Your *kamera*?"

"Oh yes!" As much as I could sit here staring for hours, we came here for a reason and I set about pulling out my tripod, changing lenses, and setting the exposure before trying to capture the picture that will launch my career.

CHAPTER 23

ÆRLEN

I STEP BACK AND watch as Cathy works.

Her eyes are bright with wonder, and even I, who have seen the lights many times, look back up at them as if seeing them for the first time. Her joy is infectious. But they are nowhere near as beautiful as she is.

Her pale skin changes colour with the lights and for a split second I wish I could strip her naked and watch them play across her belly, her arse, her tits, but then sense gets the better of me.

It is fucking cold out here. Still, my body aches for her, but I cannot give into my urges this time. This is for her, to give her time with her thoughts, and as I remind myself of that, I retreat to the shelter and sit under its sloped, moss-covered roof.

Watching her work, watching the constant smile light up her face is a torment, when I think that this may be the last time I ever see it. I make sure to bank the memory away. If she chooses to leave and has all memory of me wiped, then I must remember for both of us.

By the Norse Gods, I want her to stay. I want to wrap her up in furs and take her to a *hytte* I would build just for us, making love to her every second I could, but...I sigh. I cannot keep her here by force. She would hate me and that would be worse than losing her. Forcing a mating bond on someone is not a true bond and any feelings would rot instantly. Besides, what kind of leader would I be if I had to force a woman to be with me?

No. I just have to sit and watch her in bittersweet torment as I wait for her decision. After a while, she sets up her camera and tripod, aiming the lens at the sky, and with a final check, presses the button and turns around.

At first, she can't see me, and I watch with a selfish pleasure as panic passes over her face, but then her eyes find mine and she smiles.

"There you are." She crosses her legs and sits beside me.

"I watch you work," I say, my voice a croak. "You are a wonder."

She laughs and nudges my shoulder, her head still turned towards the heavens. "I am nothing compared to that." I swallow and gaze at her face.

"*Nei*, you are more."

Slowly, her head turns to mine. We are only a hand's span apart and I want so much to lean in and kiss her, but I stop.

She shivers suddenly and I curse myself. She is cold. I start to move.

"*Det er kald*. We must light fire now."

She stops me by setting her hand on mine. "No, the camera is on a long exposure, if you change the light now it will ruin it."

"But you *fryse*." She is so close, her scent fills my nostrils. It overpowers me and I feel my cock stiffen. Cathy hasn't noticed but shrugs and places her hands on my thighs, spreading them, so she can sit between them.

"Then keep me warm."

I move to make her more comfortable. Heat rises in my cheeks as she leans back against my chest, and I know she must be able to feel my hardness pressing into her back, but she doesn't say anything, only wraps my arms and my tail around her.

As she watches the light, I concentrate on trying to breathe normally, especially when she starts absentmindedly stroking the furred tip of my tail.

Gods! It's so sensitive, and with my already heightened emotions, I can barely suppress a grunt. Cathy pauses, and

I am certain she is going to pull herself away, when she shifts, lets go of my tail and, to my surprise, lets her hands wander to the fastenings of her trousers.

She keeps her eyes on the lights, but I notice the change in her breath, her scent, as she unpops the button, takes off her mitten, and slides her hand between her legs with a sigh.

I can barely breathe with want as I watch her rub herself, her chest moving with the rhythm of her strokes, her breath turning to moans and pants. I am so hard now it hurts.

"Ærlen..." she breathes, her breath pluming in the air. The aurora above us is forgotten as she removes her hand and reaches back, pressing her hand to my cheek. Her fingers are right beside my nose and the sweet scent of her sex lingers on them.

I groan and let out a deep breath as she guides my larger hand into the warm entrance of her trousers. I can barely get one finger down there, so I lift her slightly with my other hand and she wriggles the fabric lower, parting her legs so I have access.

As I rub her clit with one hand and reach further down, inserting two fingers from my other inside her slick opening, she leans her head back against my shoulder and gasps. She bucks her hips in time with my working hands and I am almost blind with desire.

Suddenly I feel something wet on my earlobe and pause.

Faen i helvete!

She is sucking my earlobe, scraping it with her teeth as I fuck her with my fingers. My hands speed up as I fight to control myself. I want her, I need her and as if reading my mind, she cries, "Fuck me, Ærlen!"

I don't need asking twice. In one swift movement, my hands are out of her pants, and tipping her onto her hands and knees. As she pushes her trousers down, exposing that gorgeous, milky white arse, I unleash myself. I pump my cock a few times as I stare down at her, letting my precum trickle onto her crack before I rub my tip against her now swollen folds.

"*Faen!*" I breathe. I'm not even inside her yet and I am already so close. But it's too cold to savour the moment and she reaches down between her legs, playing with her clit desperately, looking at me over her shoulder.

"Ærlen...please!"

Hearing her beg for my cock tips me over the edge and I can't hold back any more. I ram into her tight cleft and her relieved scream chimes with my own discordant grunt.

Fuck! She feels so good, opening for me, welcoming me. I pull out and smash back into her with more force.

"Yes!" she pants. "Keep going!"

I oblige. Her pants intensify the more I thrust into her, harder, faster, just how she is asking me for it.

She is so close, I can hear it in her voice, and so am I, but I have to keep going, for her. We are fucking so wildly, the air around us is filled with our fogged breaths and the sound of skin slapping against skin. The edges of my vision start to go black as I feel my release coming.

No, I have to slow down. But I don't have a chance. With a scream of pleasure, Cathy clenches around me, hard, fast and tight. Her orgasm chokes my cock and forces my own out of me with a growl.

I pulse into her with slower, deeper thrusts, wringing every drop of seed from my balls into her warm, accepting cunt. I lean forward, bending over her, and kiss her head. She tries to crane up to kiss me back but is barely able to move. I could stay like this forever, holding her, loving her, but the damn cold creeps in and I pull out and tuck myself away as she quickly wriggles back into her pants. There is an awkward silence as we compose ourselves and she goes to check on her camera. When she looks back at me with that beautiful, beaming smile, I hate myself for crushing it.

"Cathy," I murmur. "We should not do this again."

Chapter 24

Cathy

"Excuse me?"

My voice is shrill, my shock undisguised. What the fuck is he talking about? We had just had the most romantic, not to mention mind-blowing, sex of my life, letting me see not only the Northern Lights but stars as I came.

"Why, exactly? I didn't hear you protesting just now!"

I sling my camera bag over my shoulder and cross my arms under my chest defensively. There is something about this conversation that is ringing eerily familiar. Like the one I had had with Ed that time we had hooked up after we had broken up. I had thought he was coming to apologise, to beg me to take him back, but no... He just used me and then ditched me all over again.

I feel the sour saliva of dread and regret dripping down my cheeks and swallow as Ærlen runs a hand through his thatchy hair, making it stick up even more.

"*Ja*, I want to do it. I will fuck you forever if you ask me. I want you the second I see you taking pictures at river. *Guder*, I want you *nå*, but I try to keep my distance."

My jaw drops. "But why?"

He takes a step towards me as my lip wobbles and almost roars in my face, "Because you will leave me!"

I swallow. What is he saying? He can't possibly have feelings for me in such a short time. No, this had to be desperation talking. His people were on the edge of extinction, weren't they?

"You need humans. You need us to carry your troll babies, don't you? What is stopping you from keeping us all here, if it saves your people?"

Ærlen takes a step back as if I have slapped him, raising a hand to his chest.

"Is this what you think of me? That I keep you here against your will?"

Guilt and shame smash into me. That was a horrible thing to say about a community that had shown us nothing but kindness.

"No, no of course not, but..." I search for the words, but he shakes his head and disentangles himself from my flimsy grip.

"What kind of male, what kind of Jarl am I, if I force you to be mate, force you to carry children? *Nei*!" He breathes heavily and as his shoulders sink, I see something dim in his eyes. "Perhaps it is best for you to return to own kind. You do not *feel* the same as I."

He turns his head and looks out over the valley, leaving me standing there with tears streaming down my face.

"That's not fair," I croak, taking a shaky step towards the edge. "You said this was my decision and so you do not get to tell me what I feel."

I see his shoulders tense as my foot crunches on the icy rock underneath, but he doesn't look at me.

"You do not know what is best for me, just as you don't know that I have no one to go back to, no one who cares for me, no one who..." My voice cracks. "...loves me."

He rounds on me then, hands spread wide before him. "Each time I see you, smell you, touch you... I start to love you."

The last of his bellow echoes around the valley and my shoulders slump at his words. He loves me? He half crouches, gripping his hair with both hands and growling with frustration as he wrangles with his emotions. Then he straightens and flings an arm back at the shelter.

"Why you think I sit there, away from you? I not want to influence your choice." He stomps about on the platform, his erratic breaths pluming in the frigid air. "If you want to leave, go back to humans...human man maybe... I do not want to stop you."

"There is no one for me back home. But *you* actually want me to stay? Not just to give you babies...you *want* me?" My voice is small now. Perhaps he doesn't. Perhaps all that lovemaking in the cave and up here was all just...for fun. I shake my head, fighting back tears. No, that can't be true. He has told me how much he needs a mate. I gasp. But does he actually want one?

He launches towards me and grabs my arms, squeezing tightly.

"*Ja*, I want you to stay. I never feel this way before, no huldra, no human that I have watched from far. You have magic, Cathy. You bewitch me. You say, you not ready for mate and children. I respect this. If you want to leave... I *must* accept." His voice cracks and he rubs my arms gently as tears form in my eyes at his words. "Even if it means I never love again, then I will live with it, because I know you are happy somewhere."

I shake my head. "But then you will never be Jarl. Everything you have lived for...dreamed of..."

Ærlen shrugs. "Dreams are nothing, without you."

I can't take the swell of emotion bubbling up inside me and I wrench myself free, turning away from him to stare up at the same lights we had just made love under, wiping my tears away angrily. No one has ever spoken to me like that in my life, cared for me so much that they would forsake their happiness for mine. The thought of his pain tears at my heart.

He sits on the edge of the rock face, his legs dangling over the side. He turns his head and looks out over the valley, leaving me standing there with tears streaming down my face.

I take a step towards him and look down as the toes of my boots hang over the edge. If I lose my balance now, that would be it. I would fall to my death, and then the papers would be right. My parents and Ed would receive the correct information.

But I don't want to die, in reality or on paper. I take a deep breath to calm my tears and slowly sit myself beside him. Even though he doesn't look at me, he reaches up to help me into a safe position, encircling my waist with his tail as an extra precaution.

"I came on this trip to get away from reality for a time. My life had fallen to pieces and when I returned, I was supposed to start again, in a new town, a new job, new friends and a new me..." I reach over and lace my fingers through his. Finally, he looks in my direction, first at our interwoven fingers but as I speak, his gaze rises to my eyes.

"What if...my new life...is here, with you?"

He squeezes my hand and his lips part. "Is that really what you want? You not just saying this to make *me* happy, thank me for saving your life?" I hear the terror in his voice and shake my head, smiling a little to put him at ease.

"I would have thought the rampant fucking was thanks enough...don't you?"

I let my grin widen, sparking a shy one of his own, and nudge his shoulder with mine.

"But... I want it to just be us for a time. No Jarl, no babies. I want to know *you*, Ærlen."

Then I stand and hold out my hand.

He takes it and rises, pushing me back from the edge as he wraps his arms around my waist, pressing every inch of his body against me.

"And if you not like Ærlen?" He bites his lip, the tip of his fang pressing into his plump lip adorably.

"I like what I have seen so far. You are kind, loyal, honourable... But if it comes to that, then we will deal with it later. For now... Let's see how this goes."

He nods his agreement and leans in for a kiss and for one blissful moment, I am weightless. This is what I want with my life, to be held by this troll, but I push him away and turn to walk back down to the village.

He spreads his arms out at his sides questioningly as I look over my shoulder coyly.

"Well, come on then. We have to ask your Jarl not to retire just yet, to give us the time to figure all this out before you take over."

Ærlen breaks into a smile and runs towards me. He sweeps me up into his arms and kisses me once again, slowly, sweetly, before holding out his hand to lead me down the mountain.

EPILOGUE
CATHY

IT IS LATE, BUT the kiss of the midnight sun warms me and the horn of wine in my hand is dulling the ache of my newly inked mate mark on my upper arm. I look around and see the faces of my friends, some old, some new, smiling with happiness for me and my mate.

I smile back and look at the band of rune-like patterns, identical to those on Ærlen. The sage mother sets down her needles and wipes away the last of the blood from his green skin.

"There," she sighs, groaning as she straightens her crooked old back from its stooped position. "One mating bond and one mark of Jarldom."

She waves a hand to Haldor. "It is done."

The old troll smiles and hobbles forward on his cane, grabbing Ærlen by the hand and pulling him to the front of the platform in the centre of the village. Gone are the traces of mid-century technology now, gone the quaint, knitted cardigans. If any unsuspecting human wanders into Heimli now they will think they have stumbled through a portal into a fantasy realm. A large bonfire roars and trolls and huldra, small nisse and other creatures of myth I have now learnt are real, are dancing around it to the beat of wide drums, tipping horn after horn of alcohol down their necks. The streets are lit by flaming torches, a wild boar roasts on a spit, the scent wafting over the inhabitants. They are clad in their traditional garments, their best, which in the heat of the summer isn't much, and the few humans present have adopted the style.

I join Ærlen at the front of the dais and look out over the merriment, noticing that more than a few couples are engaging in dances so erotic, it may as well be called foreplay.

Watching them makes me hot and I glance over at Ærlen, whose hand is being raised above his head. He has been stripped to the waist, his defined muscles clearly on display, a crown of long grasses on his head and a matching grass kilt slung low over his hips. I swallow. He is gorgeous, powerful, and I can't wait to rip that skirt off to consummate our mating bond.

"Troll, huldra, Hidden Folk." Haldor's voice carries over the hubbub and the drums stop, every face turning towards the platform. I try to cover myself from roving eyes, as I, too, am dressed in naught but a grass skirt, a mossy cloak resting on my shoulders, and two broad leaves over my nipples, but Ærlen takes my hand and pulls me close. His eyes are heavy with want as he takes in my outfit and my newly inked mating bond.

"It is my greatest honour to introduce you all to your new Jarl and Jarlfru. Ærlen and Cathy. May they rule over you wisely, and bear many young to ensure our kind's survival. Three cheers! Hurra hurra hurra!!"

The cheer that erupts from the crowd is deafening. I don't think it can get any louder but then Ærlen grabs me, dips me backwards and plants a long, deep kiss on my lips.

"Come now, *mate*...it is time."

I grin up at him and let him lead me off the platform and away from the party, deep into the trees.

It's a bit of a climb, and by the time we reach the stone altar, the midnight sun is at its lowest, sending shimmering rays over the tops of the mountains on the other side of the valley.

The altar is perfectly framed in the orange glow of the nighttime sun.

"So...what now?"

I lean into him as heat pools between my legs. I am so turned on it's crazy. As I remember how everyone else was coupling off at the party, a sudden thought strikes me.

"Ærlen, did they put something in the wine?"

He grins and rips off his grass skirt, exposing his already erect cock. "It is tradition...in case the mating couple are a little nervous..." He shrugs, speaking slowly so I can follow, my Norwegian skills somewhat lacking. "And to spread our joy to everyone else."

He takes the moss cloak from my shoulders and spreads it on the stone altar before laying on top of it, his hands behind his head and his dick sticking up into the air, proud as a flagpole waiting to be dressed.

A sudden, all-consuming need for him swamps me and I clamber up onto the stone table.

"So, how does one consummate a bonding then? Doggy style, missionary, girl on top?" I punctuate my words by kissing up his legs, coming to rest at his bulging bollocks, licking them gently and laughing as he jumps.

"It is consummated as soon as both of us come, that's all. We can do it anyway we like."

I sit up and pretend to think, tapping my chin with my finger dramatically.

"Well then... Why don't we start how we did all those months ago..." I crawl up him and when my crotch is over his face, I turn to face his cock.

"Mmmm," he rumbles underneath me, wrapping his arms around my thighs and pulling my hips lower. "*Ja takk.*"

I jolt as his long tongue reaches out and flicks my clit, but he uses my movement to pull me lower, spanking me with that tail of his wickedly. As he starts to lap, I fold forwards and take the swollen head of his cock in between my lips. A trail of precum graces my tongue and I groan. Oh fuck, he tastes so good.

As I suck him to the same rhythm he laps at me, I run my fingers up the swirled ridge, up and down until he starts groaning into my pussy, the vibrations making me moan in turn.

Then I grasp him hard and start to pump, opening further, taking him as far back into my mouth, my throat, as I can. My muscles spasm around him and he bucks, but I hold on fast, even when he inserts two wide fingers into me, fucking me as he licks.

It's getting harder and harder for me to hold on as he works me, but I suck and lick and pump him for all that I'm worth, his frantic groans music to my ears.

My toes start to tingle, and a familiar sensation creeps up my calves, the insides of my wet thighs, and I can't focus any more.

His cock slips from my mouth as I cry out for more and Ærlen responds. My back arches as I shatter into pieces, but in my writhing orgasm, I hold onto his cock, pumping it frantically with my movements.

My release triggers his and as I sit back to catch my breath, the tip of his cock erupts with pearly white cum with such force that it shoots towards me, covering my chin, my neck, my tits with his hot, salty spunk.

Even though I have already come, Ærlen still pulses his fingers inside me, and as I clench down on them, he whispers, "Rub it on."

I obey and in the darkest part of that summer evening, I sit back on him and rub his cum all over myself, covering myself in him, letting it set into my skin, so that any who see or, as is the case with trolls, smell us, will know that I belong to him, just as he, with my juices all over his face, belongs to me.

We collapse into a heap and he takes me in his arms, kissing me deep, despite the mess we are both in. I don't know how long we lay there in the light of the midnight sun, but eventually I prop myself up on my elbow and trace my finger over his washboard abs.

"So, does this mean we are mated now?"

Ærlen nods and flicks one of my nipples playfully. "It does... There is no escaping me now."

I laugh and let my hand trail lower, following the line of hair down past his hips. He stiffens at my touch.

"You couldn't get rid of me even if you tried," I warn him, letting my hand slither between his parting legs to cup his balls. "But..." I give them a squeeze, relishing the close-eyed expression of arousal on his face. "Perhaps we'd better do it again...just to make sure."

I giggle as he growls and flips me onto my back, leaning over me with his fangs bared.

"This is a good idea; we need to make sure." His rumbling voice sends a shiver down me as his teeth graze the skin of my neck. "But this time, I'm going to fuck you like a Jarl!"

"Oh, please do!" I gasp and eagerly spread my legs, welcoming him in.

THE MONSTER LAYER'S APPRENTICE

Episode 1

Well, this was not how I had envisaged my final moments: naked, tied to a rock, my arse in the air, and a deadly monster prowling around. Prowling closer in the darkness and taking a good old sniff.

Well, if it gets any closer, the only thing it will be able to smell is the contents of my bowels as I shit myself.

"Fucking idiot!" I chide myself. The words come out as a bark while hot, angry tears drip down my cheeks.

This was all my own fault, of course... Well, mine and *his*... That damned beautiful stranger that had turned up in town with his gorgeous hair, lute and nimble fingers. Let's just say those fingers did not simply pluck at his instrument, if you know what I mean.

Now, whilst sex out of wedlock is not a crime in Fabelia, sleeping with something not human sends you on a one-way path to being the next sacrifice.

But how was I to know all that silken black hair was hiding two very pointed, very elven ears?

He'd done a runner, of course, and so here I was, tied to a rock, laid out, bare for the thing that had been stealing the village's sheep.

It's probably just a wolf, you say, but trust me, when you see what was left of those poor creatures, limbs tossed into the tree line, organs scattered around the fields, you know that ain't no wolf. Not a normal one, at least.

I try to blot the images of the carnage from my mind as a throaty growl punctures the silence.

My eyes are closed and I whimper as fear finally takes hold of me. For all my bravado, or stupidity, more like, teasing the mayor that I would rather fuck the monster than him (at least then I'd be satisfied by a big enough cock), the reality of my situation hits home. I am going to die.

I hear the padding of enormous paws approaching, the grunt and snarl as it sizes me up and then the rush of warm, stinking breath on my face.

Wrenching my eyes open, I find myself staring into the narrowed black ones of the most enormous wolf I have ever seen.

"Oh, Goddess..." I gulp. "Nice doggy...nice—" The snap of its jaws shuts me up instantly.

I try to remain still as it sniffs me, its muzzle going low between my hanging breasts. I press my lips together to stop any sound coming out but then yelp as I feel the hot, wet tickle of a tongue on my nipple.

"Hey Fido!"

A voice calls out from behind the creature and its head snaps back and out of my cleavage. For one split second, we glance at each other, mutual confusion etched on our faces, but then the beast swings round with a growl, swatting me in the face with its bushy tail in the process.

I spit the hairs out of my mouth and crane my neck to see who was bonkers enough to interrupt... whatever was going to happen to me.

And my jaw drops.

There in the clearing, the light of the moon bathing her, is the sexiest woman I think I have ever seen.

She slinks forward, curves rolling, the trinkets and tools on her leather belt clanking as she unties it and throws it to the ground.

"You want to play, Fido?" She smirks at the giant wolf, who I now see has more... human aspects to him, like washboard abs, thighs to die for and — my eyes widen — a rapidly growing cock that is pushing out from a bed of fur between his legs.

The beast growls and crouches low as if he is about to pounce, but stalks closer, sniffing intently.

The woman shucks off the grey druid's robe, exposing her voluptuous body, her long lavender hair falling over her breasts.

She looks up at me and makes a quick gesture with her hands. The manacles binding me snap open and clatter to the rock, a sound that almost makes the monster turn back, but my rescuer grabs it by the muzzle and—

I cannot believe my eyes; she has just shoved a varg's muzzle between her legs and is stroking it.

"That's it, Fido. You take a good long sniff." She widens her eyes at me and mouths, "Go!"

I don't need telling twice. I stumble from the rock, scraping my bare flesh in my hurry, and run to the tree line.

I am safe, I am alive, I am...

I stop in my tracks. That woman put herself in danger for me. I can't just leave her.

But what can I do? I am weak, naked, and unarmed.

I fall to my hands and knees in the dim light and scrabble in the fallen leaves. Then, just as I hear a moan from the clearing, I wrap my fist around a branch thick enough to be a club.

"I'm coming!" I whisper and run back to the tree line.

I stop short and the weapon I had so desperately searched for falls to my feet.

My rescuer is sat on the sacrifice rock, legs splayed, hands back supporting her, as the varg licks her.

His enormous tongue is licking her from crease to clit, rough and hard and eager.

The woman's head is thrown back and from my hiding place, I can see the sheer pleasure on her face as she moans.

She grasps the varg's fur, patting his head as he eats her, telling him what a good boy he is.

What the fuck?

Now, you might assume this reaction of mine is to the scene before me, that I am horrified that this woman is receiving cunnilingus from a deadly humanoid wolf...but you'd be wrong.

The 'what the fuck' is because my nipples have become stiff and hard, the breeze teasing them, and my core is thrumming.

I reach down and insert a finger into my cunt.

"Oh, Goddess!" I gasp as I clench around myself. I am soaked, slick, and incredibly horny.

I shoot my eyes back to the sacrifice rock.

My rescuer is on her knees now, in the same position I had been chained before, arse up, but the difference is, she is there willingly, made ready by the varg's tongue for his...

My jaw drops as I catch sight of its enormous, now fully erect dick. Just as I am wondering how it will fit, my treacherous core betrays me and clenches. Shit... I have to do something about this.

As the varg positions himself, my rescuer wiggling her buttocks to further entice him, my fingers find my clit.

A noise fills the clearing, sending birds from their nests, as he slams into her, grunting with relief, her moaning with the sudden fullness and me joining in as I rub in time with the creature's rhythmic slaps.

As his pelvis slams into her arse, it sends a ripple up her body, her ample curves shuddering with the aftershock, her heavy breasts swaying forward between her outstretched arms.

"Yes... Yes!" Her voice is low, husky and lilts with pure pleasure.

The varg speeds up now, and so does my finger, and I'm having to clutch at the tree for support. Finally, with a howl to the moon, the beast shoots his seed into his prey and slumps over her as she cums around him.

They remain motionless, as if locked together, but I am still burning, still desperate for release, so I press my back against the tree, my head tilted to the canopy and finish myself off.

My own orgasm crashes through me and wrings a cry from my lips before I can slap my hand over my mouth to stop it.

Quickly, I peer back into the clearing. Did they hear me?

The woman is sitting up now, stroking the monster's head as he pants in her lap, looking more like a docile puppy.

"Good boy, Fido... You needed that, didn't you?"

The varg looks up at her with wide eyes and whimpers.

She nods her head and makes a shushing sound. "I know. I know. So far from home, surrounded by these humans who don't understand, all you want is love."

A whimper and I feel suddenly guilty at having been so terrified... But no, these varg massacred our sheep, these monsters were killing people.

"Will you let me take you somewhere you can be safe? Where creatures of the other realms live in peace?"

I don't catch the beast's reaction, but the next thing I know, my rescuer is on her feet, pressing her head into his muzzle as if saying goodbye and then...

She zapped him.

I know, I know that sounds strange, but she picked up her walking stick, tapped him on the nose and zapped him inside the glowing purple gem at the top!

How could an enormous creature like that just disappear?

I am still pondering this as the witch or whatever she is picks up her grey robes and shrugs them on, lacing them with a leather corset that makes her plump breasts bulge over the top, and fastens all her other magical accoutrements to it so they hang over her rounded hips.

She lowers her shoulders and gives a satisfied sigh before turning to the tree line. She is staring straight at me.

"Enjoy that, did you?"

Fuck. I have no choice but to come out from my hiding place, my tail between my legs, my previous want dripping down my thighs. But I sniff and raise my head. I will not let her make me feel ashamed, not after what I have just seen *her* do!

"Who... What are you?"

The woman smirks.

"Is that anyway to thank the person who just saved your life?"

I cross my arms and raise my eyebrow, before remembering I'm still naked and dropping one hand to my crotch.

She shakes her head and gives another small sigh before spreading her arms wide and giving a low curtsy.

"I am Gisela, the Monster Layer."

Acknowledgements

I HAVE BEEN A lover of monster romance for some time but was never really brave enough to try my hand at it.

That was until I met some of the most wonderful people in the bookish community. They have all been so encouraging and inspiring and I could not have done it without them.

Firstly — to Finley Fenn. Without Orc Mountain, I would never have realised how much I enjoy these big brooding monsters. Also, for encouraging me in a DM (under another name) when I voiced my interest in writing my own series. To have the encouragement of such a big voice in the industry really made me want to make my dream a reality.

The next and most important thank you goes to Rhea Fox author. We were thrown together for the Indieverse competition and thank goodness we were! Not only did you push me into making this happen, you were the first eyes to see my work, and you inspire me daily. You helped me to get a foot in the door of the monster romance world and have become not only a valued colleague but a friend.

Thank you to Kris from A Fictional Escapist for Alpha reading, even though this may not entirely be your thing.

I want to thank my Beta readers, Mel of Bookfairymel, Mia Elliot of author_mia_elliot, Isis Quinn of mrs.pend ragon.pages and Monica of bajabule_books. You gave me excellent suggestions to make Adjusting Focus better and your encouragement was just what I needed at such a vital part of the publication process. I have plenty more stories for you and consider you valued members of my team.

Thank you to Nirav of hobbysparrow_ for the incredible cover art. I have always loved your art and now I have some of my own! You have really brought the characters to life!

Thanks go to the artists who have produced work for the promotion of this book on social media, Rio Lint of rioline_art, Jule Petrichor of petrichor.ocs and spoopysamuel. I LOVE all the interpretations of Ærlen and Cathy!

Thank you to my editor, Rachel of Bard and Butter. I hope you had a good time editing something a little...different.

I want to thank my husband for humouring my dreams of trolls in all their compromising situations and allowing me to bring them to life.

And lastly, thank you to you, the reader, for taking a chance on a new author, a new series and picking up this book. I do hope you had a good time Heimli with the Hidden Folk and that you will come along for the ride and find out what happens with Lauren, Izzy and Sam.

www.ingramcontent.com/pod-product-compliance
Lightning Source LLC
La Vergne TN
LVHW010639200726
843507LV00011B/1727